Alice M. Diehl

Griselda

A novel. Vol. 1

Alice M. Diehl

Griselda
A novel. Vol. 1

ISBN/EAN: 9783337066895

Printed in Europe, USA, Canada, Australia, Japan

Cover: Foto ©Andreas Hilbeck / pixelio.de

More available books at **www.hansebooks.com**

BY

THE AUTHOR OF "THE GARDEN OF EDEN,"

ETC., ETC.

IN THREE VOLUMES.

VOL. I.

LONDON : F. V. WHITE & CO.,
31 SOUTHAMPTON STREET, STRAND, W.C.

1886.

COLSTON AND COMPANY, PRINTERS, EDINBURGH.

GRISELDA.

CHAPTER I.

PURE white snow everywhere. Lying thick on the hill-tops against the slate-coloured sky, in drifts on the fields, where the hedges were mere lines in the whiteness, in patches on the red tiles of the village-houses — snow clinging to the grey church-steeple, clustering upon the green ivy, which was black in contrast to the

dazzling, sparkling crystals — snow melt-
ing slowly from the sloping roof of the
vicarage close by.

It was a wintry Christmas Eve at the
little village of Crowsfoot, in Midlandshire. Crowsfoot nestled in a grassy
valley under the Langton Hills. There
were farms here and there about, but no
village for three or four miles. The
small population of Crowsfoot consisted
of farm-labourers, a few tradespeople to
supply these with bread and living necessities; the doctor, Mr Mayne,—and the
vicar, the Reverend John Black.

There was no squire; there were no
'gentlemen farmers.' The Crowsfoot
folk were rough and ready, living from
hand to mouth. A hard, toiling life, but
pleasant because it was lived out in the
lap of Nature. And ignorant — stupid,

perhaps, as those hard-handed, rough men and women were, there was the charm of Nature upon them, the rude sweetness of her big babies that have never been weaned from her bosom.

When 'Parson Black,' or 'Parson,' as his rural flock called him, came to live among them, there was a tinge of savagery about these tillers of the ground. He felt it, and determined to tone it down.

John Black was strong in soul and body. He had been a friendless orphan of mysterious origin ; he had never known exactly how he came to be one of the struggling, passionate atoms called men. He had come into consciousness, living with an old nurse and her husband, but treated by them as their superior. It was 'Master John' with them, and they waited upon him, not he upon them. Their name was Hobbs; but he was 'Master John' till he was fetched away to school—a strict boarding-school, where he found, to his astonishment, that his name was 'Black.'

Self - contained, thoughtful, naturally surly, his school-life would have been unhappy had he not worked with all his might, carried off prizes, plodded upward doggedly till, as captain of the school, he won a scholarship and went to Cambridge. Here he continued his persistent efforts, took a good place among the wranglers, and went in for Holy Orders.

His life had been utterly friendless. Except poor old Hobbs and his wife, he had neither kith nor kin. He had known no father's pride, no mother's tenderness. When he won honours, there was no one to be pleased. If he had an illness, no one cared. He might have died—he sometimes told himself, with a desolate sensation which is a bitterness happily known to few in this world—he might have died, and it would have been as if a fly had dropped dead from some wall upon the ground.

Little wonder that he looked beyond this petty world for his life! They called him the 'star-gazer.' He had certainly one peculiarity—he had never learned to laugh. Happy mothers teach their loved babies to laugh, as they sprawl, young monarchs, upon their gentle knees. But John had not had a happy mother, nor had he been a loved baby. He neither laughed with his lips nor in his heart. Therefore he was a 'wet blanket,' a 'kill-

joy'—at cricket, or boating, or football
—in fact, at all those times when those
who have learnt happiness practise it,
and when those who have not, wonder
what it is, and slink away abashed at
not knowing such a simple thing. John
Black could read Greek as if it were
the plainest English ; but happiness—oh,
that, he confessed, ' floored him ! '

As he was not one to be checked or
worsted, he determined to conquer this
great science of Nature, which he considered quite as necessary to him as
mathematics. He had grasped difficult
problems most closely when explaining
them to others ; so he reasoned that he
might possibly learn this glorious un-
attainable thing, which flushed dimpled
cheeks and brightened eyes, and made
creatures sing and dance and love and

be patient, and which seemed the very essence of young life,—by watching and assisting at its birth in others. After pondering, he concluded he could do this best as a minister, or priest, or clergyman, or parson, as even he, from old Hobbsian habit, called the interpreter of heavenly matters. He had thought of being a doctor, but, as his nurse Hobbs expressed it, 'hadn't no call that way.' 'No,' he resolutely said to himself, 'I will doctor their souls and cure miseries.' And so he did.

Although without relatives or friends, he was, strange to say, not without a solicitor. The firm, Messrs Everest & Everest, of Lincoln's Inn Fields, had paid Hobbs and his wife for taking care of 'their client' in his infancy; had paid 'their client's' school-bills and the trifling expenses not covered by his scholarship during his college career. When John Black informed them by letter that he was about to enter the Church, he received a formal reply that any fees could be had on application. Once, and only once, did John have an interview with these lawyers. He intended to find out who he was and where his money came from. All he could discover from these gentlemen, who were coldly polite, as to the merest stranger who might have called upon them without pre-knowledge or introduction, was that he, John Black, had four thousand pounds, of which they were the trustees. Where that money came from, or who had placed it in their hands, he could not find out.

That hour was the crisis of his life. The waif, the discarded creature, the disowned, utterly alone, must either hate mankind or love them. He endured a brief agony of shame, resentment, desperation, and came out of it full of pity, sympathy, compassion, ready to forget self and fight for others— in fact, a real, honest, good man.

His sound heart was felt through his gruff, ungainly manner. People began to feel instinctive confidence in him. One of his former tutors, now a country parson, invited him to stay, before he began to look about him for a curacy. The delicately pretty Evelyn Vane, this kindly clergyman's eldest daughter, was greatly interested in John. The interest became love—strong, deep love on John's part. Mr Vane did not object to John's peculiar position, so John Black and Evelyn Vane were married. Messrs Everest & Everest made no demur about providing the necessary money; more than this, on his wedding-day, John received an intimation from them that he would shortly be appointed to the living of Crowsfoot, in Midlandshire, a living which was worth some three hundred and seventy pounds yearly.

'These Everests are not the stones they would have us think them,' was John's idea. He had a stern simplicity about him. With him it was wrong or right, good or bad. He saw no middle paths, and was absolutely free from suspiciousness. But Mr Vane, double his son-in-law's age, had seen mankind without a veil. He knew now that behind the Everest protection was the mystery of John's birth and parentage. But he kept these notions to himself.

After a short honeymoon in the Highlands, John Black and his young wife returned to install themselves in their future battle-field. They had to fight ignorance, semi-savagery at first. The people of Crowsfoot had been neglected. The living had been one of many held by one man. It was looked after by any curate who chose to bury himself temporarily for a consideration. There was no school. Children tumbled up as they best might till they were big enough to work, when they went into the fields. They looked upon church as they looked upon carriages and servants, — as something belonging exclusively to the rich ; and they were very poor. The church, when John Black 'read himself in,' was literally in ruins. It smelt of damp, like a vault. No one had been forthcoming to mend the organ, so there was a poor old wreck mildewing away in a corner. The very cover

to the Communion-table was in rags. At
first John was raging; he was possessed
with anger and indignation till he had hard
work to control the outward man—to seem
calm. Evelyn, his wife, respected his
righteous wrath. She agreed with him
to put aside half their income till matters
were mended. Then both—steadily, earnestly, patiently—began to stem against
this tide of idle, wanton neglect. The
church was repaired. John went the
round of the parish. He went into the
cottages as an old friend, come to help
everybody and fight their battles for them.
His firm hand grasped the toil-worn hands
with a grasp of possession. Once their
hands were grasped, their hearts soon
followed John's strong, tender heart. He
was no apostle, no saintly idol, among
them. He was not even their shepherd.

No—he was the head of the flock, leading them as one of themselves. As such, he soon led them in the right path towards happiness. Dirt, idleness, listlessness and their attendant vices gradually dropped away. On this snowy Christmas Eve, seven years after John Black's instalment as vicar of Crowsfoot, there was not a more thriving, prosperous village in Midlandshire.

Yes, there it lay, half-buried under the snow. The two chubby little boys born to John and Evelyn Black during those seven years had been busy in the frosty garden making a snow man. The vicar was out; he had gone to a farm some two miles away, where the house-mistress was dying. Mrs Black and the one old servant were so busy preparing the Christmas meat and puddings for the poorer parishioners, that they had wrapped the little boys up like mummies, and had sent them out to that great enjoyment of childhood, wallowing and messing in the snow, to be rid of them.

What a pleasant kitchen was the kitchen at Crowsfoot Parsonage! It was small, but the walls and ceiling and floor were so white, the pots and pans so bright, the crockery ranged on the dresser shelves so shining and spotless, every tiny bit of steel on the big grate so brilliant! Now a glowing red fire was urging the pots to hiss and boil. There was a warm odour of hot pastry —Jemima, the plump servant, had just drawn out one batch of smoking, light-brown mince-pies from the oven, and was pushing in another tin. Mrs Black, seated at the table, was rolling out paste with her delicate thin hands. She had the face of an angel, the village-folk said. And, though thin and pale and tired— for the vicar's active helpmeet was in delicate health, and little Doctor Mayne had been 'dropping in' by his request very often of late — there was a true spiritual beauty on the fair face and in the tender blue eyes of the mother of those bold boys who were shouting outside.

'There is someone at the door, Jemima,' said Mrs Black, as Jemima shut the oven-door with a clang. 'Go and see; there's a good girl.'

Jemima hurried out, and came back round-eyed with horror.

'It's young Wright. Says his mother's dead; but don't you go for to believe him, ma'am.'

'Oh, dear!' Mrs Black was out of her

chair, through the passage, and at the open door in a moment.

There, on the stone pavement outside, stood a great boy in a smock-frock, blubbering. He had gone home from his farm - work in the middle of the day, and had found his mother on the floor lifeless. He had hoisted her on to her bed, covered her up, and rushed off.

Mrs Black was accustomed to be ready at a moment's notice.

'Run for Doctor Mayne,' she told the lad, ' and I will be with your mother as soon as ever I can.'

She seemed to make one spring back into the kitchen. She collected brandy, beef-jelly, cordials into her basket, giving Jemima rapid orders the while. Then she flew upstairs, regardless of pain, of loss of breath. She had tied on her bonnet, had wrapped herself in her huge grey soft shawl, and was back again in the kitchen before the old servant recognised what her mistress's intentions were. Then she stood aghast. She knew that Mrs Black took an intense interest in this poor soul, who was slowly dying of consumption. But she did not dream that the vicar's wife would risk going out to-day thus in her precarious state.

'Why, you are never dreaming of going out, ma'am?' Jemima lost her breath from horror, and stood gazing at her mistress as if petrified. 'Master'll be back directly, or I'll go.'

The maid implored, coaxed. She well knew that the vicar and Doctor Mayne were both anxious about Mrs Black, whose energy seemed to grow stronger as she grew weaker with a weakness brought about by overwork among the people and in her home. But the more Jemima fumed, the more determined her mistress became.

'Nonsense!' she said. 'A bright winter's day like this! It will do me good. A matter of life and death, too!' Then she gave a dozen different orders, and hurried off down the back garden towards the gate leading to the fields.

The sky seemed clear, it was true; but a slight breeze was scattering the snow from the branches. Behind the vicarage, a bank of heavy grey clouds was slowly but steadily rising. As she trod the narrow gravel path where the man who attended to the Vicar's cob and to the one cow had swept aside the snow, a bird gave a gasping chirp and fell at her feet. It was one of the poor robins who came to the window for crumbs. She picked up the panting bird, and called 'Tom—Harry!'

The little boys left their snow man and ran to her. She bade them take the poor bird indoors, and put it in a little box lined with wadding, near the fire.

'There are lives to be saved to-day,' she said, so gravely that the red-faced little urchins were sobered.

Long after, they remembered that day, and how they stared after their mother as she hurried away over the untrodden snow, across the field, she and they so unconscious of the terrible meaning of her words. The little lads' boisterous spirits were gone. They went quietly into the warm kitchen with their bird.

'Lawks a daisy! You don't mean to say as you've brought a dead robin into the house?' said Jemima sharply, as she bustled about. 'I ain't one for old wives' tales, as your dad calls 'em; but I'd sooner see corpse-lights a-hoverin' about them graves in the churchyard!'

However, 'mammy's' orders were law; and Jemima, feeling that life was suddenly going askew on that particular Christmas Eve, helped the boys to lay the shivering little bird on the wool, and let them squat on the corner of the broad fender watching the little heaving red-breast and the filmy round eyes, while she went uneasily about her work getting their tea.

'Your dad is a time!' she said, as she clattered the teacups and cut hunks of bread-and-butter. 'You'd better have your tea here, and get it done.'

Shades of coming twilight were gradually settling upon the snowy landscape outside. Although the glare of the snow made a white light of its own in the kitchen, warmer red reflections on the bright copper, pewter, and tin utensils from the leaping flames were ruddy, cheery spots in the pleasant interior. The boys clambered to their seats on either side of the kitchen table, and, while they buried their noses in their mugs and gnawed at their bread-and-butter, they kept up a subdued chatter —subdued, because Jemima was 'worried' —the vicarage term for tempers and humours incidental to humanity.

'I seen him flutter a wing!' mumbled curly-haired Harry, with three-year-old grammar.

'He's all right enough!' said Tom,

with the superior wisdom of knicker-bockered six. ' By the time mammy comes back— Halloa, there's snow ! ' he suddenly shouted. ' Jemima, it's snowing ! '

Both boys shot themselves upon the kitchen floor, and clambered to the window-seat, and with noses flattened against the panes, were staring out watching great soft flakes fluttering to the ground before Jemima—who, with the excuse of ' seeing to the parlour fire,' had been to watch for her returning master—came back.

' Hurrah ! It's snowing ! ' The quickening snowfall meant a bigger snow man, finer snowballs, to the boys. In their joy they forgot Jemima's ' worry.' Tom was just shouting—' They're bigger than the feathers out of mammy's bolster that

day we played at sea-serpent,' when he
turned and saw such a grey horror
on Jemima's face, that, after pausing
one moment, he slid down and set
up a howl.

' It's enough to turn the mask of one's
blood to see you two a-gloating over
the snow and your mammy out in
it,' said Jemima, with deep disgust,
which completely upset little Harry,
who followed suit and began to sob
and cry. 'Ah, you may well cry!'
And in the anxiety which hardened
her against the lusty boys, who took
all their delicate mother's devotion as
a right, and who seemed so brutally
unconcerned about her so long as they
had all they wanted, Jemima left them
to sob and cry.

She went to the front door that opened

upon the lane. As she did so, a gust of wind came dashing the whirling, circling snow into the narrow passage. The sky was inky black above the white hedge opposite. No sign, no sound of the returning Vicar, or of any other human being.

She went back to the children in dismay. The snow was coming down with a vengeance now, twisting, curling, and drifting. In a few minutes it was many inches high on the kitchen window-ledge.

'Can't see 'im now,' said Tommy, in a subdued voice, alluding to the snow man.

'No, nor you won't see yer mammy neither, if this goes on!' said Jemima. Then, immediately repentant, she went and cuddled the boys, and, kissing their scared little faces, told them she did not mean what she said.

' The angels come out nights like this to look after them as can't look after themselves,' she said. ' There—go and see to your bird ! He's flutterin'.'

But the two small faces were glued to the cold window - panes, watching for angels.

' If they're goin' to look for mammy, p'raps they'll fly past here,' suggested Harry. His elder brother was absorbed in thought, gravely sucking his thumb.

Then came a sharp rapping at the door and sounds of voices. Jemima, running, opened the door. There stood the tall Vicar, stamping the clinging snow from his high boots, and calling out, ' Mind you don't forget the warm mash, William, , and give him a regular brisk rub down,' to the man who was dimly visible through the falling flakes trying to lead the steaming horse with the chaise round to the stables through a drift which had collected during this last bad half-hour.

'Shut the door, quick, there's a good lass!'. The Vicar came in, contentedly shook the snow from his macintosh, and hung it on its accustomed peg. Then he walked briskly into the kitchen, this tall stalwart man with the square face, dark hair, keen though kindly eyes, and firm mouth.

'Dad, dad!' The boys were down and about his knees. The confidence brought about by their father's presence cast away thoughts of angels, robins, and a benighted mammy. But he kissed them and put them aside.

'Where's the mistress?'

Jemima incoherently related the afternoon's occurrences. 'She would go, master—she would go!' was her refrain.

'You say young Simmonds went for Doctor Mayne?' As Jemima nodded assent, John Black walked out of the kitchen, put on his macintosh, thrust his clerical felt hat over his brows, and went through the beating snow to the other end of the village, where the doctor lived.

The neat little house came upon him suddenly, as it were, with its brown door, red lamp, and well-swept frontage. Even the laurels loomed greenly in the whiteness, Doctor Mayne's gardener having shaken them free from their snow burdens an hour before the storm began, and the chill gusts of wind continuing to empty the glossy leaves. John rang the clanging night-bell, and was impatiently shaking the snow from his hat, when the door opened, and there stood the cheery little doctor, with his round face redder than ever.

'Halloa! Mrs Black none the worse, I hope?'

The Vicar's heart sank suddenly, unaccountably. He was always fighting against superstition in others. Now he was unexpectedly called upon to fight it in himself.

He walked in, shut the door.

'Where is my wife?' he said.

'Where—is—' stammered the doctor, amazed. Then, with the readiness which is an absolute essential in a medical man, he went on, 'Why, Mrs Black is at home long ago, of course!

She left poor Mary Simmonds some time before the snow set in. Come in—'

'And have a glass of wine,' he would have said. But, as he saw the strange expression, the sudden pallor on the Vicar's face, he stopped short, and added, 'Perhaps, though, she did not go home when the first flakes began, but took shelter half-way.'

The Vicar shortly said that there was no house on the lonely road between the Vicarage and Mary Simmonds' cottage.

'She is not home; we must go and look for her,' he added.

'Certainly, my dear fellow.' Doctor Mayne, trying to conceal his misgivings, —that delicate creature, with a time of trouble imminent, out in weather like this!—hustled on his thick coat. 'I will go with you. We had better go in my gig.'

'We cannot get round — she went across the fields.' There was anguish in the Vicar's voice.

'My dear sir, we can get round by the waggon-road that leads through Rawkins's fields to Watt's Wood,' said the doctor. 'We had better have the trap.'

He gently forced the Vicar into his consulting-room, then went off post-haste, ordered the gig and his pluckiest mare, and, with his wife, who was in consternation at the thought of Mrs Black, 'in her state,' lingering or lost in the snow-storm, packed blankets, brandy, and a hot bottle under the seat. In the bottle was beef-tea, which was a perennial *pot-au-feu* at Doctor Mayne's.

The Vicar, as the brave little mare
went struggling through the storm, knew
nothing of these preparations. It was
all the two men could do to keep seated.
The shrieking wind carried heavy masses
of snow hither and thither, as it went
howling across the white fields, roaring
in the tall tree-tops, raging among boughs
and chimneys, catching up whole hun-
dredweights of snow and, fiercely wield-
ing them as a weapon, dashing them
against hedges or gates or other obstacles.

'She's a brave old gal!' said, or rather
shouted, the doctor, as the mare stemmed
against wind and snow, and dragged the
gig over the drifts and through the loose-
lying mounds. 'She'll do it!'

They called at the vicarage, found
that Mrs Black had not returned, and
then urged the panting, labouring horse

up the lane which would bring them near to the fields the Vicar's wife must have passed through on her way home. Between the gusts they caught sight of the white slopes, bare, smooth, unbroken by a footstep. The pathway was buried. Doctor Mayne grew more uneasy. 'I wonder where she is?' he was just thinking, when the mare stopped dead.

They cheered her on; the doctor shook the reins, tickled her smoking flanks, then got out and tried to lead her. It was of no use. The black mare stood with drooping head, as if she were riveted to the ground. Not a step would she move. Doctor Mayne smoothed and patted her steaming sides; she only shivered. He lifted up her hoofs and looked for stones. There were no stones, and, as he replaced her listless limbs, there they remained.

'She's done up!' said the doctor. 'The only thing I can suggest is for me to wait here while you explore.'

'But you will be snowed up in a few minutes,' said the Vicar, springing down. They were on the brow of the slope, exposed to the full fury of the storm. He looked this way and that. He hardly dared remember that she, his wife, so loved, so closely bound up with his life, till it sometimes seemed as if she were never less than part of his very soul and body—was somewhere, somewhere—here —in this dead cold, this biting wind, this heavy, freezing snow.

'I can be dug out,' said Doctor Mayne. 'Go—go, man—go through the woods to Simmond's cottage, then track her homewards. When you call out, I will go to you; then, if necessary, we can

carry her here, and, if I turn Bess round,
no fear but that she will go fast enough
towards home!'

Track her? How should he track her?
There was the skeleton copse through
which he must pass to reach the cottage.
One look, and with head steadily bent
down, he literally burrowed his way
through the deep-lying snow, stumbling,
for here it lay perhaps two feet thick, and
half-a-dozen yards farther on was up to
his elbows. He flung himself over the
stile and was on comparatively free
ground. Then he ran—ran as if escap-
ing from an enemy, and in a few minutes
was knocking at the cottage door.

The door opened.

'Mother's better, sir,' said the lad,
looking surprised to see the Vicar in this
weather. Mrs Black had revived the

fainting woman, and had left her comfortably settled for the night. The little sitting-room, with its homely furniture— its neat bed, where the invalid was lying on the pillows as the Vicar's wife had deftly piled them, its Dutch clock ticking steadily away in the corner—looked cheery, comforting—coming upon it suddenly from the external bleakness, as the Vicar did.

He stepped quickly in, shut the door, and, after a word to the sick woman, asked for his wife.

'Lor', sir, she left this two hour ago! She's home by this time.'

'Which way did she go?' John Black's voice was hard, stern, in his anxiety.

'It wor fine enow when she started,' said the lad, frightened at the Vicar's abrupt manner — he who was always so gentle with his poorer brethren. 'Doctor'd been here a couple of minnits —ay, less nor that—then off she went down by Mrs Jones', Nurse Jones', to get her to stop th' night wi' mother.'

The Vicar went out, shut the door, and left young Simmonds all agape, looking after the striding figure as it disappeared into the white cloud. It was coming down more heavily than ever — and she, his delicate flower, in this! John Black forgot all in his one wild hope that she might be at nurse Jones'! Doctor Mayne might wait there on the hillside—there was more at stake than the snowing up of the doctor and his black mare. Down the hilly lane he rushed, meeting the storm, dashing the blinding snow from his face with his half-numbed hands—down, till, in his fierce haste, he leaped the garden gate.

Nurse Jones, a gaunt, but pleasant-looking widow, had just come in from seeing to a sick person in the village, and was shocked to hear from her son's wife, with whom she lived, that Mrs Black had been there and would not be persuaded to stay. She was drinking a cup of tea, and revolving in her mind whether she should go out into the storm again to follow the delicate lady, when the Vicar rushed in, and, looking wildly round, cried,—

'Good God!—Mrs Jones—where is she?'

The three started up—young Jones was there. Nurse Jones, seizing a shawl and tying a comforter round her head, said cheerily, though inwardly dismayed,—

'She's been and gone, sir. But I'll stake she took shelter like somewhere. I'll lay we'll find her in that old barn in the captain's field. 'Tis a snug place on a day like this. Here, Luke, you get out the lantern, and bring a couple of blankets. We'll be down the lane and through the gap in the hedge and across that ploughed field in next to no time. Don't you come, Mary.'

While she talked, she pushed the Vicar gently towards the door. Then she was off into the snow with huge strides. Nurse Jones boasted she'd be off to a patient as quick as anyone else could ride.

'But the barn is a good half-mile out of her way home!' came in a tone of anguish from the tall figure speeding along beside her.

'Ah, we women-folk ain't like the men, sir. We ain't so fool-hardy. Mrs Black knowed that a bath of this sort of thing might be bad, like she is — and, though she don't care for herself—-thinks less of herself than I do of that oid cow of mine Farmer Watts giv' me when his missus got better of the fever—-she's got it in her heart to think of them as has got to come after — the little uns.'

But even while she spoke, as if Mrs Black's delay were of little or no moment, Nurse Jones had mis-givings. She had thought the Vicar's wife looking unusually ill. Even to her strong nerves, the idea of the tender - hearted little wife and mother everyone loved so — fainting, falling, and buried under these cold drifts— was a strain. As they turned into the field where the old disused barn was, and she saw the blackened tumble-down structure looming darkly through the giddy mass of falling white atoms, she shuddered. She fancied the doors were shut. If Mrs Black were not there—what would it mean?

She must spare the Vicar that awful moment of calling into dark silence and hearing nothing but his own voice.

'You stay here, sir, please, and watch for Luke with the blankets—'

Without another word she ran on-wards.

The doors were shut! Padlocked? No, 'Thank God for that!' she said, as

her chilled fingers fumbled with the door.
Oh, why were they numb, dead, just when
she wanted them most? She rapped with
her knuckles, put her lips to the crack of
the crazy door, and called, 'Mrs Black,
Mrs Black!'

Again she tried the door. Then she
cried out loudly. Then she put her ear
to the rusty keyhole.

Heavens! What did she hear? That
curious little cry—not a bleat, not a chirp,
not a whine, but one she knew so well
that it set all her blood leaping with eager
energy, and, almost wild with different
feelings, she gave one strong tug, and
stumbled into the barn.

.   .   .   .

The Vicar waited impatiently under
the trees. There was a certain comfort
in the knowledge that Nurse Jones had

gone on ; he fully saw the necessity of
waiting for Luke with the lanterns and
the blankets—still, it was a cruel experience. He stamped about ; he tried
to stifle his fears, to believe that, all
this while he was ferreting in the snow,
that dear wife was safely home. He
tried to think of comforting words he
had told his fellow - strivers from the
pulpit a few Sundays back—just after
the frost set in, and many would be
out of work — that it was the shorn
lamb which felt the tempered wind, the
labouring ewe that was gently led by
Providence, the forsaken plants, and the
homeless birds that were housed and
fed, no one could see or find out how.
Only it was so!

'Dare I insist upon this to others,
and not believe it myself ?' John Black

asked himself, with anger at his own
perturbation. He looked, peered through
the falling snow, but he could not see
the barn. The moments seemed hours.
He prayed with all the passion of his
soul that his one love—his only friend,
his wife—might be spared to him. It
was a time of temptation, struggle; but
he gained the battle. When young
Luke Jones came up to him in the fast-
growing darkness, he was calm.

They went along, the lighted lantern
casting fitful rays about. As they came
near the barn, a voice was heard shouting, 'All right!' in a triumphant feminine tone. The Vicar stopped short.

'God forgive me!' was the short
prayer that went up to Heaven. Then
he knew—he had not suspected it—that
in those recesses of the soul which are

never rightly known by human perception, he had doubted, almost despaired, of the very Providence he had steadily preached to others.

But there was some excuse! This wife of his was the one woman in his whole life. He had not known mother, sister, or feminine relation. So soon as earliest childhood was over, he had almost resented the homage of ignorant, matter - of - fact, but well - meaning Mrs Hobbs. Evelyn's love had come to him, a sudden heaven; and he had thought she was lost, killed. God would forgive him, 'worm though I am, and no man,' he thought in his new abasement, as he and Luke struggled towards the barn.

'You must not come in yet; here, give me that lantern and them blan-

kets!' That, in an extremely every-day,
business-like tone of voice, was the
order given by Nurse Jones, who took
in the lantern and the armful of woollen
wraps, and disappeared.

'Oh, this is all nonsense!' said the
Vicar, roused, reanimated. 'Keeping me
from my own wife indeed!' He tried
the barn door. It was fastened from
inside. He knocked impatiently.

'You must wait a moment, sir, if you
please,' called out Nurse Jones' voice,
pitched at its most peremptory height.
'I'll come to you presently, safe enough.
Mrs Black's here all right; but we can't
let you in just now.'

'Oh, very well!' said the Vicar. He
supposed his darling had been wet
through, and that the nurse was rub-
bing her into warm life again, or some-

thing of that sort. He drew his coat closer, crowded down his hat, and leaned up against the barn door, advising Luke to do the same. 'Let us present a fair front to the enemy, my boy,' he said, in the hilarity of sudden relief.

The wet, cold snow pelted them more unmercifully than ever as night came on.

'How I am to get the mistress home I don't know!' said the Parson.

Luke, in his slow bucolic way, was suggesting that he and his wife could sleep on the cottage floor, and that Mrs Black was more than welcome to their little room under the thatched roof, when the Vicar started,—

'Good Lord! what was that?' he said. He felt his hair bristle on his brow. Fear, wonder, hope, joy—all crowded upon him.

Then the barn door scrooped, and
Nurse Jones said, 'You may come in!'
in that queenly manner she assumed
at crucial moments in the lives of
families, when women are all, and men,
if not exactly nothing, are 'next door
to it,' as she could have said.

And Parson John Black stepped out
of the snowstorm into the dim barn.
The lantern on the floor lighted up a
corner, where he saw Evelyn's sweet,
pale face among a pile of blankets, hay
beneath her, hay around her.

'Before you go to her, look at your
dear little daughter, sir!' said Nurse
Jones proudly, uncovering the bundle
in her arms just enough to show a
sweet little pink face, like some pretty
rosebud, in her rough wraps. 'If she
hadn't ha' been the dearest, patientest

little soul, you'd ha' been a widower now, instead o' having the sweetest little daughter on the face of the earth. Now don't you go making a fuss with the mistress, sir—she's got to stop here yet-a-while. But we'll make a fine bedroom o' the old barn afore we've done. And we don't care for snowstorms, nor for nothing, now that we've got two, instead of losing one !'

Nor did the Vicar care. And he thought that the moment when he reverently knelt by the side of his wife, lying so sweetly contented on her bed of hay, the happiest moment of his life.

'Baby was so good—oh, so good, John!' said Mrs Black, as her husband took her chill, frail hands into his warm strong ones. 'I could not have believed that it was in a tiny, unconscious creature to be patient like that.'

It was the patience of the little infant, prematurely born in a barn, that led John Black to name his one and only daughter—Griselda.

CHAPTER II.

THE babe born in the barn that snowy Christmas Eve was to live.

They called her 'Griselda.' She was a quiet, patient infant. She never, during the first five years of her little life, had much attention. For the tender young mother, who would have been as devoted to her first girl-babe as she had already been to her sturdy sons Tom and Harry, was an invalid.

Mrs Black did not rightly recover

from the exposure to the cold that
night when Griselda was born in the
snowstorm. She became gradually paralysed. When Griselda was six years
old, she was helpless, carried from her
bed to her sofa by her husband, and
dependent upon Jemima as a child upon
its nurse.

John Black's right hand—his helper,
his active second self—was physically
dead. But her sweet mind and bright
brain remained. Mrs Black's sofa in
the Vicarage parlour was the centre
of the house. The Vicar and Jemima
planned and worked together for the
fragile creature. Tom and Harry, rough
boys though they were, trod softly, and
hushed their loud young voices in the
house for mother's sake.

John Black bore his trouble well—

and not well. He said nothing about it to anyone. Outside his home, he was more brusque, more commonplace. Within his home, he was gentle, firm, tender, and worked unceasingly. Up at sunrise, he got his reading and writing, and his sons' lessons for the day over, often before breakfast. Then came a precious hour devoted to his wife, when all the strong wealth of love in his deep nature was lavished upon his stricken darling. His parish duties were fulfilled to the letter. But there was something wanting. People said that John Black was 'not the same man at all.' They felt a change, though they could not describe it. The outward change had a deep-seated cause. John Black rebelled against his fate. His deepest feelings—those that belonged to him as a creature in Eternity—were bitter, hard, daring. He bore his cross in sullen anger.

Life at the Vicarage had proceeded quietly for six years. Mrs Black's condition was an accepted fact. People were kind, sending books, flowers, and newspapers, and presents of game and fruit. The proud Lady Romayne, of Feather's Court, would often send over a groom on horseback with some little delicacy. Then came a time—a time of change.

It was spring. Mrs Black lay on her holland-covered sofa in the neat little drawing-room which Jemima kept carefully arranged and dusted. Choice hothouse flowers were in a china bowl on the centre table. A spreading fern hid the little grate. The children had

been for their morning ' talk to mammy,'
as they called it. 'Mammy' was a little
tired. But it was a pleasant languor
rather than actual fatigue. As her
gentle blue eyes wandered from object
to object—all her little treasures, her
girlish possessions, her wedding-presents,
carefully placed where she could see
them to the best advantage — she
thought how kind everyone was,—
how good it was to live. Then, as
she looked without into the glorious
sunshine, and saw the great chestnut
trees a blaze of bloom, and the trees
in the orchard showered with delicate
pink and white blossoms, she felt it
would also be good to die. If there
were such peace, such beauty in this
little world, they must exist in other
globes among the countless millions of

planets as well. She listened to the
children's voices in the orchard,—to the
bleating of the young calves staggering
knee-deep in the waving grass, to the
busy twittering of the parent birds busily
feeding their young — the hedge between the Vicarage and the field was a
favourite resting-place with the birds,
—and she was perfectly happy.

Meanwhile, an adventure was hap-
pening to little Griselda in the orchard.

Griselda's life was not all pleasant-
ness and peace. Jemima was fond of
her nursling ; but Jemima was always
busy,—her work was rarely forward, and
never over. So she grew brisker and
rougher, and Griselda's bathings and
dressings were times of torture. The
fair child had long, beautiful golden
hair. Jemima had a quick way of

combing out the tangles which was positive anguish, and brought the tears to Griselda's eyes. She bore this patiently. How it had come about that she had a sense of being in some way a culprit—of deserving all that was bad and nothing that was good—was a mystery.

Perhaps it was from her father's manner to her, which varied and was constrained, or from stray confidential sayings of Jemima to her village friends in her presence, alluding to her as 'poor unfortunate little soul!'—or perhaps it came from Harry and Tom's imperious ways.

They liked their pretty little sister, but she was their victim and slave. They played with her instead of with the old dog, because, when the old dog felt he was being taken liberties with, he snarled and bit, and Griselda only shed silent tears. They used to bind her with the clothes-line, and carry her about, pretending they had captured a robber or bandit. They knocked together a little go-cart, and would rush about the garden dragging it at full speed, with Griselda crouching in it, till it capsized. Often and often she was scratched and bleeding. She was always a mass of bruises, for which Jemima called her a naughty tom-boy. For Griselda never betrayed her tyrants' secrets. They would haul her up into an apple-tree, and go off on some mischief or another, and she would sit there quietly, perhaps softly singing to herself, or thinking beautiful thoughts about the clouds — those wonderful round white glories sailing across the blue sky—or dreaming over a fairy tale.

For 'mammy' read fairy tales to them sometimes in her sweet, weak voice. She wished the children to believe there was more in the world than hard, common, every-day life. She fancied—poor lady — that stories of knightly prowess might give Harry and Tom a sense—a vague sense—of chivalry, and she knew that a romantic soul looked through those blue windows, Griselda's eyes. But the knights' exploits only made Harry and Tom more warlike. It was Griselda who was comforted by the old tales. She dreamed that a prince came and delivered her from her brothers. The dream became an idea, and, dwelt upon in those lonely hours among the apple-branches, grew to be a belief.

He would not come, she fancied,
till Harry and Tom had grown far
more cruel. But he would come, she
felt sure.

To-day her brothers were in their
wildest humour. Griselda, sent out into
the orchard to play upon the daisied turf,
went off quietly to a corner, with an old
doll with a battered nose, and pins instead
of the glass eyes the boys smashed in long
ago. Its wig had departed the first day.
Its gauzy clothes had been torn up for
a kite-tail. The mutilated effigy was
wrapped in one of Griselda's old pinafores, and was about the most miserable
apology for a doll that ever was. But
the child loved it with a deep passionate
love—battered nose, pin eyes, bald pate,
and all.

She was a picture, as she sat there

on an old horse-cloth, her delicate oval
face with the great wondering blue eyes
and the grave sweet mouth peeping
out from her blue cotton sun-bonnet,
her little figure like some huge flower
against the background of rough red-
brick wall. She was watching the
boys holding a mysterious conversation
as they stood by the tool-house. The
gardener had forgotten to lock the
door when he fetched out his scythe.
She watched Tom, a plain dark lad
with a hard forbidding face, hand out
two spades to curly-haired Harry with
dismay. What was he going to do?

She soon found out. Tom came
across to a bed, lately made for some
cuttings of peach and apricot trees promised to the Vicar by a richer neigh-
bour who had a fine assortment of

wall-fruit, and began to dig a deep hole near the wall. When she asked what it was for, he told her to mind her own business. So she sat clasping her doll tightly to her little heaving chest, suffocated with dread lest Tom should mean to bury her doll.

The idea of parting with her 'baby,' as she called it, was so dreadful that it was almost a relief when Tom stayed his digging, and, throwing off his cap, for he was hot, told her,—

'If you particularly want to know what this is, it's your grave.'

'I may have baby buried too?' lisped Griselda.

'Oh, yes; and then there'll be an end of the horrid ugly thing!'

As Tom glanced contemptuously at the doll, Griselda thought hopelessly

that there would be an end of her
too. She wondered what it would be
like, to lie in that hole and feel the
shovelfuls of earth coming down upon
her body, till she was covered in, and
the blue sky would be gradually shut
out, and how long it would be before
her body changed and she flew out.
The Vicar had once shown her a new-
born butterfly struggling out of its
chrysalis shell, and had told her that
dying was like that. The dead people
he read the service over were the mere
shells ; they had changed and flown up
to a beautiful place, where they would
live, far more lovely to look at than
the most splendid butterflies. Griselda
believed everything she was told. She
did not know a lie. So she knew
Tom would bury her, because he had

said it; and she knew she would fly
out again like that butterfly flew when
his weak wings were shaken free, because her father had told her so.

Still, she felt sad. Mammy would
miss her. Jemima would not be bothered with her washing and dressing
and clothes-mending; but when she
thought of that hearty kiss—of that
honest 'God bless you, my darling!'
after Jemima had tucked her into her
little bed at night—she was sure
Jemima loved her, and would be as
sorry that she was dead and buried as
she herself would be if her doll-baby
were taken away.

It would be better if Tom would
change his mind. Or perhaps someone might come! Then she would
certainly not be buried!

She sat watching the green door in the red wall, and listening breathlessly. She heard distant sounds of opening and shutting of doors. Then she heard Jemima's voice, and another which she did not recognise, then footsteps, the click of the lock of the door in the wall.

She stared, amazed.

A lad, younger than Tom, dressed in a dark-green velvet riding-suit, stepped down into the orchard—a handsome lad, with dark-curling hair. He wore high leathern boots and a fantastic low-crowned green velvet cap, which he touched lightly with his gauntleted hand as he saw Griselda.

'I am Hal Romayne,' he said, with a stare of his dark brown eyes at these children, who looked to him as rough as any of the village 'cads.'

Tom stopped digging, and said, 'Oh, are you?' — looking the intruder up and down. Tom had his ambitions. He had heard of public schools. He had hated young Romayne for his father's wealth and position before he had seen him. He hated him, now he did see him, for his dress and his good looks and his slight manner of haughty condescension.

'I have come from Lady Romayne to ask your sister to spend the day at Feather's Court to-morrow,' Hal Romayne said, carelessly playing with his hunting-crop, and thinking that Griselda's face was the prettiest little face he had seen. 'Will you come?' he said to her.

Griselda had stood up, still clutching her old doll. 'Are you the prince?' she asked with awe.

'What prince?' Hal Romayne smiled encouragingly upon this little maiden with the quaint ideas and the silvery, innocent voice.

Griselda went to him, and, standing on tiptoe, whispered,—

'The prince come to save me from Tom and Harry.'

Hal reddened, and stared disgustedly at the boys, who did not look inviting to his fastidious taste in their rough clothes, flushed, with soiled faces and hands. Hal had delicate white hands, which he kept white with the most zealous care, and, if there happened to be a speck upon his linen, it was rejected as unwearable.

'Are not your brothers kind to you?' asked young Romayne, loftily protecting.

'They want to bury me — and my baby too.' Tears welled up into Griselda's eyes. The corners of her lips drooped and quivered pathetically, as she nodded her head towards the grave.

'I don't suppose they would have hurt you,' said Hal, with an air of supreme contempt. 'Do you always amuse yourself frightening your little sister?' he said, in a drawling way, to Tom. Then he offered his hand to Griselda. 'Come indoors to your mamma,' he said. 'She is to say if you may come.'

Griselda went with this extraordinary being who had suddenly appeared in her life. Hal cautiously handed her up the steep step, closed the garden door after them, still holding her little hand;

then they walked side by side along the narrow garden paths, between the tall lilies with their close-shut green buds — between the bushes of moss - rose, which next month would exhale a wealth of perfume from their pink round blooms, Griselda, gazing at her prince, arrived at last, in a species of ecstasy. They walked through the narrow passage into the drawing-room.

Mrs Black looked up with a faint smile as they came in—the tall, well-dressed lad and her little Griselda in her rough cotton frock and old sunbonnet. Outwardly an incongruous pair ; but the delicate lady had perhaps grown to be a dreamer in her suffering solitude. She thought no more of Hal than that he was a fitting escort for her little maiden.

She had determined to refuse Lady
Romayne's invitation for Griselda.

'Griselda is too young to go out,'
she said to the boy, amused to see
how his face fell at her remark. 'You
know she's only six years old.'

'But I will take care of her,' said
Hal valiantly, his dark face reddening.
'I assure you, Mrs Black, that no harm
shall possibly come to her. She shall
be my special charge.'

Mrs Black was amused. Little Griselda at Feather's Court! The notion
was absurd. But there was some peculiar power about that boy. She
hardly knew she had consented before
he had taken leave—a courtly farewell—
and had mounted his pony, and had
ridden off, followed by his attentive
groom.

He doffed his hat and bowed low as he passed the Vicar in the village. John Black glanced back, and wondered at that boy.

'A strange lad!' he mused. 'Whatever did he mean by that Don Quixotic business?' He wondered still more when his wife told him of Lady Romayne's invitation. 'Whatever can have put it into her head?' he remarked. 'Griselda at Feather's Court! Too ridiculous!'

He grew grave when he heard Mrs Black had accepted. But his wife's decision was his law. Griselda was destined—or doomed to make her *début* in the fashionable world early in her simple life.

CHAPTER III.

JOHN BLACK, that very day
when Griselda and Hal Ro-
mayne first met, happened to
be in very good spirits. His humble
friends seemed unusually prosperous.
At the smithy on the village green,
Hugh Wells, the blacksmith, had come
out, his swarthy face broadly smiling,
'to tell t' parson the missus had had
a letter from the son out in "Australy."
He was gettin' on capital at the sheep-
farming. Says we shouldn't know him
if we was to come across 'm, parson.

He's got a long beard, and weighs twelve stun.'

This was pleasant news for the Vicar, who had been instrumental in the emigration of Wells' consumptive son, when Doctor Mayne had said a sea-voyage was his last chance. After congratulating the blacksmith, and standing for a minute or two watching the lads at cricket — it was a half-holiday at school—he went on to the school, a brick building under the chestnut - trees. The door was open, and he heard scrubbing. He passed the village charwoman, who moved her pail for him, and, going through the soap - and - watery odours — which were odours grateful to his nostrils, with his hatred of dirt—he knocked at the door of the schoolmaster's sitting-room. The

schoolmaster and mistress were partly
paid by him, partly by subscription,
and the weekly pence contributed by
the parents. Here John Black spent
a happy half-hour, looking at maps,
drawings, exquisitely neat sums and
copies, the work of the rough children,
who but a very few years ago were
running about, ragged, unkempt, bare-
foot, and, if not actually in mischief,
with hopeless aimlessness. Then, coming out, he met a young woman with
a beautiful child in her arms, and
she blushingly curtseyed deeply as she
shyly, reverentially glanced upward at
the man who had been her good
genius. He had come across her two
years ago in the darkness, crouching
near a deep pond. She had been
ill-treated and forsaken by the son of

the owners of the village inn. John
heard her tale, or rather extracted the
wretched old story from her unwilling
lips; then he took her to stay at
the Vicarage to help Jemima till he
had stormed at, threatened, and shamed
the young man and his parents into
acknowledgment of a promise of marriage which had evidently been given.
He had had a hearty delight in
marrying that couple. He often had
a hearty joy when he saw the happy
young wife and mother serving in the
bar, a favourite with her husband and
parents-in-law, whom she helped and
served with the energy of grateful
love.

Strange that this day, of all days,
when he was to receive a crushing
blow, he should first be confronted

with facts that caused his happiness!
As he went through the village, noting
the neatness of the cottages in their
fertile little gardens, and remembering
what a wilderness—what a tumble-
down, poverty-stricken place this was,
but how, by docile following of his
lead, these honest folk had raised themselves and had thriven — his heart
swelled in his breast, and he began
to meditate whether indeed there was
any ill in life which could not be
conquered by good will and work.
Sin, disease, poverty, idleness—he and
the people of Crowsfoot had success-
fully fought against these.

'Of course there is death,' he thought,
with a sigh. That was the great un-
definable thing which conquered man.
He had seen them die—frail infants,

peacefully breathing out their souls;
strong men, fighting desperately with
the creeping, numbing influence; young
girls and youths, talking of life as
it fled from their weakening lips; and
he had stood by, powerless.

Curiously enough, just as he was
thinking of death, Doctor Mayne came
driving along the road homewards.
The Vicar prepared to pass the gig
with a smile and a lifting of his felt
hat; but the doctor drew up, and,
alighting, told the man to drive home
and tell Mrs Mayne he would be
back in less than an hour.

'I've been wanting a talk with you
for some days,' said the cheery, bustling
little doctor. 'But you are such a
busy man, and those long legs of
yours are like seven - leagued boots.

You're from one end of the parish to the other in a minute. There's no catching you!'

'Nothing wrong, I hope?' asked the Vicar. 'I understood that scarlet-fever case was all right, and that nothing further was threatening.'

'Oh, that's all right enough!' said the doctor. 'No; I'm just going round to the captain's; he's got a touch of the gout — that port wine again, you know—and I thought you wouldn't mind going part of the way with me.'

John Black followed Doctor Mayne gravely through the 'kissing gate' leading to one of the captain's grass fields. Gravely, because he had met this Captain Battersby, a naval captain who had retired and farmed his little

property, that very morning. The
captain was irascibly grumbling at some
labourers, but had not complained. This
visit was some excuse.

He hardly knew what the doctor was
talking about as they strolled along the
path across the fields, till they came
in sight of the old barn, when Doctor
Mayne stopped short and began speaking
about it.

'Wretched old shed!' he said almost
vindictively. 'To think what it has to answer for!' Then he went on talking about
that day when little Griselda was born.

'I never advised keeping them there,
if you remember,' he said. 'It was Nurse
Jones who frightened you about the
possible consequences of moving them.
Nurse Jones is an estimable woman in
her way. I don't deny that she is pru-

dent, clever—all that. But she is too strong-minded, to positive for me. If I had had my way, I should have had a litter knocked together on poles, and four men would have carried Mrs Black and the baby from the barn to her own room at once.'

'All's well that ends well,' said the Vicar uneasily.'

'Of course! But in this case it is not well. How could it be, with an icy wind, enough to cut you in two, blowing through those crazy planks upon a delicate creature like that? My wonder was, and is, that she ever rallied at all. By the way, have you noticed any particular change in her lately?

'She is more cheerful, more lively, and I think eats more than she did,' began the Vicar eagerly.

'Ah,' interrupted Doctor Mayne, 'I don't mean that; it is other physical signs.' He stopped; his voice died upon his lips. He had braced himself for some little time past to say to this comrade of his in the hard battle of life what he must say; but at the very crucial moment his courage failed him.

Perhaps his faltering, his hesitation, told the truth less cruelly than raw words.

The Vicar's heart gave a leap; then he felt as one feels who is suddenly, unaccountably, mortally wounded. He closed his eyes, he groped and would have fallen, but for Doctor Mayne's timely outstretched arm. The world seemed to wheel round him, while his life stopped short—stood still.

When he opened his eyes, they sought the doctor's—dazed, agonised.

'Don't let us beat about the bush,' he feebly said. 'You are going to tell me something—for mercy's sake be quick, quick!'

The doctor wiped the moisture from his kindly eyes. 'Look here, old man,' he stammered; 'you've always been talking to us about Home from the pulpit, and a good thing too—this hole of a world, with all due reverence to Him who made it, is no home for us. Well, she is going Home, and going very fast; now, you know, you've only been preaching as yet; you've got to show us—and you will too, if you hold up.'

'Is there nothing to be done?' whispered the miserable man.

The doctor looked round, as if appealing to the fair spring landscape, so full of life, to yield up some, if only a breath, to fan the waning life so precious to this poor good man.

'You might take her—by slow stages —to some more bracing spot,' he faltered. But—oh—Black, how can I advise it, when she might die on the way? Will you understand that these years since that snowstorm have been a slow dying? You have kept her alive, like a plant without roots; hers were cut off that dreadful day.'

'Don't — say — any — more!' said the Vicar, with a gasping sob. 'Thanks!'

The two men gripped hands, looked at each other, and parted.

Doctor Mayne, unstrung, 'not himself,' went up the slope to the captain's house—the cheerful white building with the gay green shutters, where he found some little relief in talking over the

Vicar's impending loss with the captain over a pipe and a glass of grog, and listening to the captain's oft-spoken remark that if he'd known that that old barn was wanted as a patent hospital, he'd have seen to it; but, as nobody told him, it wasn't his fault, he didn't guess—was it?'

And John staggered off the opposite way. He turned his back upon the barn, although it had given its rude shelter to his wife and babe in a sore strait. He went blundering on till he came to a clump of Scotch firs that grew on the knoll where he had stood waiting, while Nurse Jones went onwards, that terrible Christmas Eve six years ago. It was a bright warm evening; a vivid sunset shone through the dark pines. He flung himself down upon the spongy earth, strewn with layers of the dead needles, studded with brown cones. He was cold, sick, trembling. He dared not realise what Doctor Mayne had said — he fought off the thought of death.

'If God made Eve from Adam's rib, he made her my own out of my heart,' he fiercely told himself. 'She is my heart; I have no other. If she goes, I shall turn to iron, to stone.'

He thought back upon his lonely, harsh boyhood—upon that interview with the lawyers, who showed him by speech and manner that he was merely a matter of business, that his very existence and how it came about was a matter of business, and nothing further—upon that dreadful hour when he went out of that office, repulsed, thwarted, disowned—and

fought out the short fierce battle from
which he must emerge mankind's close
friend or desperate enemy ; he remembered his first glimpse of Evelyn, when
she came fluttering into the peaceful
parlour of that quiet country parsonage
in her white dress, with an angel's pitying sweetness in her soft eyes for the
solitary youth. He thought of the first
time her gentle arms had clung to his
neck, her fair head had rested on his
shoulder, and then he started with fear,
for he fancied he heard a terrible cry
go out from near to far and echo in
the distance.

But he had not cried with his poor
human voice ; it was only the fierce cry
of his agonised soul going up to God.

How would he declaim God's com-
mandments from the Communion - table

with his soul a rebel? How would
he preach love, forbearance, faith, hope
from the pulpit when her fair body was
lying meekly in the earth outside the
church, cold and senseless? How
could he work and sympathise and con-
sole and be patient when his house was
no home, empty, solitary? God forgive
him! At that moment the little beings
who called him father were, in his anguish, less than the dust out of which
they came, and to which they must return.

Then, with quick revulsion, a wild
hope sprang up within him. After all,
a man, a fallible man, had said this. It
was only the fiat of one human voice—
he would have the advice of the first
physicians. Everything that could be
tried should be tried; nothing that
could be done should be left undone.

But—the money to do this?

No one, not even Evelyn—the confidant of his schemes, his hopes, his perplexities — knew how hard and how difficult it had been to provide for the actual necessities at home, while he was ready - handed to meet each valid call upon his income from without. His life had been a perpetual struggle to make one sovereign do where two would scarcely have sufficed.

He would not get into debt. The children's wants had been supplied with close economy. As for himself, he went about almost threadbare. The lofty Lady Romayne, who professed to admire 'character,' had even remarked that it was a pity Mr Black went about so shabby. She really could not ask him to dine; it was more than she could risk. It was now May. He had money in hand that would, could only last till midsummer, with the strictest economy.

How were these expensive physicians to be paid? How was any plan for saving his darling's life a little longer—just a little longer—how hungrily he caught at that straw of hope!—to be carried out?

There seemed to him but one way, to sell out part of his little capital—that four thousand pounds. Until now he had merely drawn the interest.

These practical thoughts had brought balance. He went home with an aching, heavy heart; but the sharp torture was relieved. It was twilight when he walked into the Vicarage. He heard the boys' voices in the stable-yard. Griselda had stayed indoors, following Jemima about,

some inward warning telling her to avoid
Tom. She came into the passage a fair
dream-child, saying, 'Father, will you
have some tea?'

He bent and kissed her, saying, 'No,
darling, thank you;' then he went into
that bower—as he felt his wife's sitting-
room to be — sanctified by her sweet
presence.

'Oh, dear, it is you!' There was such
a soft content, such a luxury of relief
and satisfaction in that dear weak voice!

He went to her couch, as he always did;
he knelt beside her, took those frail, chill
hands in his, and leant his burning head
upon them.

'It has seemed such a long time to-day,'
she began. 'I hope nobody is ill, dear?
Your head—it is so hot!'

John schooled his voice, and gave her a

brief account of all he had seen and heard that was cheery.

'How splendid!' she said, her slight strength flickering up with satisfaction. 'Oh, John, how happy, how thankful—we ought to be—how grateful to God!'

She spoke these words—she sent home those bitter stabs to the grief-stricken man, with reverence, with loving awe.

'Yes,' he said. That was a strange sound, that 'yes,' half-suffocated, half-daring.

He dared his own emotions. He took a bold moral leap, as it were, into a higher stage, which just now he did not believe he could possibly reach, the state of cheerful resignation.

'Put your hand on my head,' he said. And once more Evelyn Black laid her thin hand on her husband's head, and smoothed his rough hair with a caressing touch. How that gentle touch had comforted him, soothed his fatigue, calmed his over-tired brain all these hard-working years! To-night it awakened a new agony, for he thought of the possible long weary years when he would have lost it—when never more in the flesh should Evelyn speak, or touch, or look at him.

He could not endure the strain. He laid her hand gently back, rose, and paced the room, his usual thoughtfulness for her comfort gone.

She thought, 'Poor dear, something has vexed him, and he is too considerate to tell me!' So she began to talk to him, with some amusement, of Hal Romayne's visit. He listened, as he always listened to anything she said, till she mentioned little Griselda. Then he started.

'Oh, don't talk about Griselda!' he said, in a tone of such anguish that, if Mrs Black had not seen her little daughter a few minutes previously, he would have alarmed her.

As it was, she merely thought he had one of his fits of hopelessness about her paralysed state, when he avoided the subject of the Christmas Eve when Griselda was born, and everything connected with it. So, after getting an impatient 'Yes, yes, dear — just as you think best,' to her demand for his sanction of Griselda's visit to Feather's Court to-morrow, she changed the subject.

After John Black had carried his wife to bed that night, he went to his study and wrote to Messrs Everest & Everest, the Lincoln's Inn lawyers.

'GENTLEMEN,—I am anxious to realise as much money as possible.'—Then he detailed his wife's illness.—'In these circumstances, I feel myself compelled to sell out at least one thousand pounds of the four thousand you have invested for me. I place the matter entirely in your hands, to sell out where and when you deem best, and have the honour to remain, —Your obedient servant,

'JOHN BLACK.'

That letter safely posted, John felt less completely miserable. In a week or two it would be in his power to do all that could humanly be done to prolong his darling's life. Doctor Mayne, whom he daily visited in the forlorn hope of getting a stray scrap of reassurance, talked of some months before the dread power, Death, could finally conquer them. John hung upon the word 'months.' Never had it seemed a shorter span, a more lightning-like flash of happiness, than it did to this man, who must — so God willed — lose his all!

But he must hope against hope; he felt that. 'If I am cheating myself, I must do it, or I cannot work; I cannot hold up my head!' he cried out within himself. So he went about his daily tasks doggedly, with a fair front, and a soul propped up with stray reasonings and impromptu fallacies.

Messrs Everest & Everest waited three days; then they telegraphed,—

'Please arrange interview on subject mentioned in your favour of 13th inst.; we should prefer it.'

In his highly-strung state he could not imagine what this could mean. His money was his own. Why hesitate —why delay—why demur?

'It has been their way, I expect, since time immemorial, and they cannot change it,' he bitterly said, alluding to the gentlemen of the long robe. Then he telegraphed back an appointment for next day.

Evelyn looked wistfully into his eyes, and clung to him more tenderly than ever when he said good-bye that morning, when he brushed up his worn clothes, tied his white neckerchief with greater care than usual, and started for town.

He said he 'must go,' but there he stopped. It was not her husband's 'way' to conceal anything. So Evelyn wondered, put two and two together, feared, and arrived at no result, except a dread lest John should have lost some of that little capital of his, on the subject of which he had always been so reserved, if not taciturn.

Meanwhile, John went express to town —went, bewildered by the noise and racket, straight into the leisurely stagnant atmosphere of the great legal quarter, and was at once ushered into the presence of the junior partner, 'our Mr Walter Everest,' as the clerks alluded to him when writing in the name of the firm.

The tall, ungainly man, whose lanky legs always knocked together, as if he had seldom or ever left the library-chair he seemed pretty well to live in through the long office hours, half rose, half nodded, half waved John to a seat, and ended by saying solemnly to the clerk who ushered in the client,—

'A chair, Mr Jones, if you please.'

Then, while John looked round with a feeling of dull pain,—for each chair, each item in the bare room—the very pattern of the carpet, and the stains upon the old blind—recalled that cruel interview six or seven years ago,—' our Mr Walter Everest' looked closely at the Vicar through his spectacles, then leisurely removed them and laid them upon the office-table before him, then said slowly and severely,—

'Mr—John—Black?'

As if, indeed, the name were not only new and strange to him, but that it was not legally proved that this gentleman here present was entitled to it at all.

'I am John Black,' said the Vicar, almost roughly, plunged back, as he felt, into these painful recollections. 'I came—'

'One moment, if you please, sir,' suggested Mr Everest, taking up a bundle of papers, and applying one corner of his spectacles to the writing thereupon. 'I have reason to believe —ah, yes, I see—that our Mr Henry Everest is concerned in this matter equally with myself; I will therefore postpone any discussion thereupon until I can ascertain that he is unable to be present.'

'Certainly,' said John. Upon which Mr Everest sounded a gong, and when a clerk appeared, and, in answer to his inquiry as to whether Mr Henry Everest was within, replied, that he

did not know, but he would see; he
ordered that if Mr Henry Everest were
to be found, he was to tell him, with
his compliments, that he would be
greatly indebted to him if he could
arrange to spare him a few minutes.

The clerk disappeared, and Mr Walter
Everest, with an air of being profoundly
occupied with some crisp new whitey-
blue papers at his right, shot a remark
now and then at John — the spring
seemed promising; he hoped the farmers would do well, etc.—until the door
was opened, a little man came abruptly
in, and, with an air of annoyance at
being thus unceremoniously fetched, said,
'You sent for me? I am just engaged
in that Butcher *v.* Butcher case.'

'I will not detain you a moment,'
blandly said the junior partner, rising

and offering his senior his chair, which he at once impatiently turned his back upon. This gentleman, a Mr—John—Black—perhaps you recollect we were trustees during his minority for a small capital settled upon him—wishes to sell out.'

'The papers? Of course you have the papers,' irritably said the sharp little man, stretching out his hand. Then there was a short silence while he flicked open some blue sheets and John's letter, which was fastened to them.

'You—are—Mr John Black?' he said almost brusquely, after he had finished their perusal.

John, who felt as if his position with these lawyers was at a greater disadvantage than ever, reminded him that it was but a few years since their interview, when both gentlemen now present refused to give him any information respecting the relations or guardians who had provided for him.

' My—dear sir!' began the little senior partner, with an evident effort to tolerate this most unlegal talk. ' Really, if our clients place matters of sentiment before us, we cannot be blamed if we respectfully decline to enter upon matters which are entirely without our sphere of action. I have some slight recollection of some previous interview ; but in the interests of business, interests which are paramount, I naturally made no mental note of an interview which had no bearing on any case I happened to be concerned with. As to this proposition of yours—to sell out part of the four thousand pounds we have in-

vested for you—we are really not in
the habit of arranging for the disposal
of such extremely small amounts. I am
right?' he added, turning to his lanky
brother.

'Certainly,' said 'our Mr Walter.'
Upon which John's heart sank.

'But, let me consider,' went on the
sharp-eyed little gentleman, poising his
chin upon his hand. 'I think, Mr
Black, we might possibly meet your
wishes another way. We are always
more than ready to meet the wishes of
our clients when it is in our power to
do so. Now, what I suggest is this:
that, as you are in want of ready-money,
you will draw upon us from time to
time, as occasion demands, up to the
sum of four thousand pounds; meanwhile, you may continue to draw the in-

terest of your invested four thousand,
which will remain undisturbed. Do you
understand?'

John Black did not. He stared. He
tried to think, to calculate, to cope with
these wily lawyers. His brain seemed
in a fog. As he understood it, Messrs
Everest & Everest were actually offering to lend him money.

He frowned. He stared into vacancy,
pondering. Meanwhile the sharp eyes
of the little senior partner were stealthily
watching him.

'At what rate of interest?' said John
suddenly, turning upon the two.

'My dear sir, we are not Jews, nor
are we usurers,' said Mr Everest, senior.
'We wish to serve you, and at the
same time to save trouble to the firm
—that is all. Of course, it rests with

you to accept or reject. As for percentage, that is out of the question. We hold your four thousand pounds. That is sufficient security for us.'

There was further talk. John Black left Messrs Everests' office puzzled, discomfited, unhinged, although with a cheque for one hundred and fifty pounds in his pocket.

'What does it all mean?' he asked himself, unable to find any explanation for the easy generosity of these cut-and-dried solicitors, who were not only ready, but pressing with their cheques.

'It is a mystery — a strange, cruel mystery!' he mused, as he returned to Crowsfoot. All the bright buoyancy of his life, since he met Evelyn, seemed obscured by a heavy cloud. If he could have seen those lawyers after he left

their office, could he have been en-
lightened ?

The impatient little senior partner
bowed him out, then, closing the door
carefully, returned to his brother, grave,
and anxious.

'He could not possibly have thought
anything, could he?' he said, in a low
tone—how different from his 'hectoring'
voice a few minutes back!—'I am sure
it must be all right ?'

'Quite so,' said the lanky Everest, in
a satisfied tone, stretching out his long
limbs, and beginning to pick his teeth.
'It was an awkward situation, very.
But you steered us through—you steered
us through!'

'To think he never suspected anything,' said the little man, on whose
features a sweet smile was gradually

spreading. 'That is what I cannot understand. The man must be a dunce—an absolute idiot!'

'My dear boy, he is a parson in an agricultural neighbourhood,' returned his brother, who seemed vastly relieved. 'It was a case of assimilating his intellect to theirs, and you know what that means, or of leaving the place in disgust. Well, he has stayed.'

'You may say what you please, Walter, but he is a fine fellow,' said Mr Everest, senior, energetically. 'That nose — so wonderfully like, you know — then that powerful chin — he will make his mark when his time comes.'

'Ay, when his time comes, if it comes!' observed his brother sardonically. 'You know well enough that on this point you and I differ.'

'We shall see,' said Mr Everest drily, as he went off.

.   .   .   .

Meanwhile, John Black was home, one hundred and thirty pounds in his pocket. The other twenty was with the great physician, Sir Geoffrey Boole, who was to see Evelyn at Crowsfoot in three days from that date.

CHAPTER IV.

GRISELDA slept very restlessly the night after Hal Romayne's visit to Crowsfoot Vicarage. She had strange dreams. She was a princess shut away in a dismal cavern, guarded by a horrible dragon, which had eyes like Tom's, when his temper was at its worst. She was weeping and mourning in her terror when Hal Romayne, dressed in cloth of gold, with a gold helmet on his long brown curls, came flying through the air on his long-tailed grey pony and thrust his spear

into the dragon, which shrivelled up
into nothing at the first touch.

Poor little maiden ! There was a
worse dragon watching at the Vicarage
doors to claim its prey — one which no
mortal eye could see, no mortal hand
could touch.

Meanwhile, her father lay awake with
his great grief, of which Griselda was
the innocent cause.

Years after, he remembered and bitterly blamed himself for his injustice to
the tender little girl. She went into his
study, the morning of her visit to
Feather's Court. Jemima had told her,
with great pride, to go and show herself to
her 'par.' Jemima had clear-starched and
ironed a white frock with minute care,
had bought four yards of blue ribbon at
the general shop in the vlllage, and had

tied up her sleeves and shining hair, besides hanging her little silver locket round her neck. Griselda had never been so 'fine.' She went to her father, blushing with the conscious feminine pride of ' looking nice. ' The woman-babe was innocently happy, till her father, who was writing, looked up, and at her.

That look she never forgot, any more than she forgot what followed—a look worse than the dragon's in her dream, for it was dark, harsh, unfathomable, expressing, as it did, the battle that was raging in the man's soul. In another man it might have meant hate; but in John Black it meant fierce struggle.

'Well, Griselda?' he said, awkwardly leaning back in his chair.

The child paused a few moments, won-

dering what it was which had changed
her father. Was it childish instinct or
a foreshadowing of the beautiful coming
woman's nature which made her forget
her own pain in sympathy for his?

She went up to him and laid her little
hand upon his knee. Her great eloquent eyes seemed to say,—

'I am not afraid of you.' Then she
prattled about her spending to-day at
' Fevver's Court ' as she called it, end-
ing almost with awe — for Griselda
thought even a halfpenny a consider-
able sum — ' the ribbon cost fourpence-
ha'penny a yard!'

'Ah,' said John Black, whose brain
was unsteady after the shock and his
sleepless night, 'pretty things cost a
lot, Griselda! You cost me'—then he
checked himself—and, passing his hand

across his forehead, felt that his mind was clouded to-day, and it behoved him to be on guard.

' Did you buy me, papa ? Did you pay' —Griselda paused to think of a large sum —'did you pay a whole shilling for me?'

John Black got up, laughed—what a laugh!—and said, ' Go, child, go!' Never before had he spoken to his only little daughter like that. She gave him one yearning grieved look, and crept away.

Jemima, when the smart waggonette drove up, and a portly nurse appeared at the door, and pompously informed her that she had 'called to fetch Mr Black's little girl,' could not find Griselda. She was not in the study, not with her mother. At last she found her sitting on the floor in the bedroom, pale, her big eyes luminous with repressed tears.

'Are you scared? Would ye rather not go, my lamb?' asked Jemima, thinking the 'darling was frightened at going out all alone.' But Griselda shook her head. So Jemima tied on her Sunday straw hat trimmed with watered-silk ribbon, and fastened her little black silk cape, then watched her drive off among the carriage-ful of smart nurses and children, like some little stray bird that had flown by mistake into a superior nest.

There were two girls, Lydia (aged seven) and Mabel (five), their nurse and nursemaid, and a handsome strong-limbed baby-boy on his own nurse's lap. This kindly countrywoman, who had children of her own far away, made room for the stranger, and, seeing that the other nurses contemptuously scanned the child's coarse clothes, and that Hal's

fashionably-dressed sisters looked askance
at her, she made the baby-boy smile and
coo and pat her face with his fresh dimpled
hands.

Feather's Court was a great castellated
grey-stone pile, with many mullioned
windows. It stood in a large deer park,
and its turrets had for background those
purple hills Griselda had longed to see
when she sat gazing at them from her
chair in the orchard. There was a moat,
now dry and full of shrubs and ferns.
When Sir Hubert Romayne bought the
estate, eighteen months ago, to please
his rich wife, one of whose ancestors was
supposed to have built the house, he found
the neglected place—which had belonged
to a spendthrift—going to rack and ruin.
He spent a small fortune on repairs and
improvements. It was now as nearly

perfect as a rich gentleman's country-seat
could be, from the wrought-iron gates and
stone lodges at either side of the park
to the Italian garden that sloped upwards
behind the Court towards the heath-
covered hills.

Griselda felt as if she had become part
of a fairy tale. She stood on the steps
of the great building, gazing upwards with
astonishment. This was a palace indeed
—a fitting home for yesterday's prince.

The little girls had run up the steps
and had disappeared into the great hall,
where statues gleamed white through the
long, narrow window panes. The nurses
were taking the parasols and wraps and
the picture-book, with which the languid
little Lydia beguiled the tedium of the
drives, out of the waggonette, while the
coachman leant back and indulged in such

complimentary badinage as he dared with Mrs Walters, the stout pompous nurse, who was a power in the kitchen-regions of Feather's Court.

Meanwhile, 'baby's nurse,' as she was called, bethought herself of the child with the up-turned wondering gaze. Had she been suddenly gifted with second-sight— had she known how, when, and in what manner this roughly-clad little maid would share in the weal and woe of the important family she served—she might have been more deferential in her treatment of Gris-elda, but she would scarcely have been so spontaneously, genuinely warm-hearted.

' Look here, Mrs Walters,' she said impatiently, turning round, the baby in her arms. ' What's to be done with this good little soul? Is she to go to her ladyship ? '

'Oh, dear me, no!' said Mrs Walters, coming panting up the wide steps. 'My lady to be bothered by a parcel of children indeed! She had better go straight to the nursery, and Mary'll look her out some old toys to play with.'

Now, a certain slumbering resentment in the baby's foster-mother against the autocrat of the nurseries was suddenly wakened into active life by Mrs Walters' words. She flashed a look at her from her fine black eyes, then she said to Griselda,—

'You come along with me, my dear.'

Griselda put her little hand into the nurse's. They went up a wide, shallow staircase between banks of rare hothouse plants, then along a dimly-lighted corridor, where fleecy rugs were spread before closed doors, and where there were cabinets and tables full of china and curiosities from foreign lands, till they came to an alcove, where the nurse pushed aside a curtain, and, after someone within had called out, 'Come in,' in reply to her knock at the door it concealed, pushed the door open, and Griselda found herself in a bright room all flowery chintz, gilding, and mirrors, where a lady was writing at a fanciful escritoire near one of the windows.

'I have brought little Miss Black to see you, my lady.'

'Oh!' Lady Romayne, a stout, florid, but good-looking woman, glanced up, concealing her annoyance at 'Porter's taking such a liberty,' for this foster-mother of her second son's must not be annoyed. Even Sir Hubert nodded to her when he met her, and praised his boy, and hoped she had good news of her children, *et-cætera.*

'Go and speak to her ladyship, my dear,' said the nurse.

Griselda went across to Lady Romayne, and lifted her face to be kissed. Lady Romayne, slightly taken aback by 'the little creature's coolness,' just touched her forehead with her lips, when she was still further astonished by the child's asking if she were Hal's mamma?

'What do you know about Hal?' she asked, thinking there was something eerie-looking about those deep, dark eyes and that pale, golden hair.

'He came to the orchard yesterday.' Griselda tried to speak very plainly, without lisping, as her mother taught her to do. 'Is he here?'—looking round.

'Hal is out riding,' said Lady Romayne. 'But, if you go to the nursery, they will give you some nice toys to play with. Ask Miss Lydia to let her play with the doll's house, Porter, or Miss Mabel will lend her a doll.'

Lady Romayne turned to her writing, thinking somewhat hardly of the Vicar of Crowsfoot for his child's 'want of manner.' 'Dressing her like that, too! Those men who are all philanthropy, and who pet up and spoil the labouring population, are just those who neglect the duties that lie at their very doors,' thought her ladyship severely, thinking that next time she was asked to subscribe to the Crowsfoot school she would tell that Mr Black what she thought of him.

Meanwhile, Griselda went to the day nursery—a huge lofty room in the new part of Feather's Court— which had large windows overlooking the marble terraces and bright flower- beds, and where there were gay pic- tures and a rocking - horse, and bears that ran about when they were wound up, and all sorts of expensive toys which had amused the children on one or two occasions, but which were discarded with disgust by them on the third.

But when it was suggested to Lydia, who was lying supine on the soft carpet, seemingly trying to bore holes in it with her shoe - heels, that she should show the visitor her doll's house, she gave a wild Indian yell, and had to be pacified. And when Mabel, the round-faced and amiable one of the two girls, brought her magnificent wax doll, which had as many fine clothes as Lady Romayne herself, and laid it in Griselda's lap, Griselda shook her head.

It was too 'grand'—she felt she could not play with such a wonderful creature —that, if she did, that pink waxen forehead might pucker into a frown, and those blue glass eyes, with the real eyelashes, flash sudden anger at her.

So she sat with her hands in her lap, watching the nursemaid brushing the girls' hair and putting on gossamer lace and muslin pinafores through the open door leading to the night-nurseries, —and listening to the nurses' talk.

'Where is she going to have her dinner?' asked the baby's nurse.

'Here, with us, of course,' said the head-nurse, just as the footman who attended upon the nurses made his appearance to 'lay the cloth.' 'She can't go down, with Sir Hubert and all there, dressed like that.'

Griselda had heard and understood, and her face had flushed—just when a boyish voice said, 'Halloa! There you are!'—and Hal walked straight up to her.

'Come along down!' he went on, taking her hand. 'What!'—for Mrs Walters came bustling up to prevent him—'going to stop up here? Stuff and nonsense! I am going to look after her. Don't any of you trouble your heads about her.'

'But, Master Hal'—the fat nurse's tone was conciliatory, for the son and heir of the Romayne's was not to be trifled with, and it was as much as any servant's place was worth to interfere with him—'she hasn't brought her pinafore.'

'Here—Mary!' Hal unceremoniously took Griselda to the open door and told Mary to 'lend her some of Mabel's things.' So Griselda went from the nursery in a pretty muslin overdress, escorted by the eldest son, who, looking critically at the broad blue sash Mary had tied round her waist, called out to ask why they hadn't put her on some better ties.

'Because she wouldn't have them, Master Hal,' said the nursemaid spitefully.

'Jemima bought the ribbon; it cost fourpence - halfpenny a yard,' said Griselda, looking up with big eyes at Hal. He looked more splendid to-day, she thought, even than yesterday. He was dressed in black velvet, with glittering steel buttons.

'How are those cads, your brothers?' asked Hal, with an air of lofty protection, as they went downstairs, he leading Griselda by the hand. 'Have they tried to hurt you?'

Griselda shook her head. 'What are cads?' she said, feeling that the word was disparaging, and that, however roughly her brothers treated her, she must defend them, even in this exalted atmosphere.

'Oh, I don't know!' said Hal carelessly. Then he opened the dining-

room door, where Sir Hubert, Lady
Romayne, the two elder little girls, the
tutor, and the governess were at luncheon, and led her straight up to his
father, saying, 'Mr Black's daughter—
papa, Griselda.'

'Well, you are a pretty little maid,
with a pretty name!' said Sir Hubert
kindly. He was a stout man, slightly
bald, very well-meaning and practical,
although not clever. His weaknesses
were his fatuous admiration of his wife,
who ruled him—and of his eldest son,
who ruled her.

'Just let her sit by you, pa, and see
that she eats something, will you?' asked
Hal coolly, walking off to his seat by
his mother. 'I think I shall take her
round the place after luncheon,' he continued, as the men-servants hastened to

offer to him his favourite *entrées.* ' Beer,
Williams, please ! I promised her mother
to look after her, you know. What dy'e
call these things ? Quenelles ? Take
them away. Mother, that cook of yours
gets worse and worse. She'll give us
nothing to eat presently. I wish you'd
get a man. Towerden says he can't eat
anything cooked by a woman.'

' My dear boy, Towerden's father is
a duke!' said Sir Herbert, smiling,
for, strange to say, he appeared to like
his little son of barely eleven to talk
like an airy young man of twenty or
more. ' By the way, my dear, isn't this
the heroine of the snowstorm story you
were telling me the other day ? '

Lady Romayne assenting, he looked
at Griselda with more interest, and asked
her if she had any brothers and sisters.

'Two—brovers,' said Griselda. Then, almost before she knew what she was saying, she added emphatically, 'Brovers, not cads.'

'Not what?' said Sir Hubert, startled, while Hal's tutor—a young B.A., whose tutorship to this scion of an ancient house was sweetened by a heavy salary —looked meaningly at his pupil.

'Oh, I know what she means!' said Griselda's prince, by no means abashed. 'I called 'em that. So they are; they threatened to hang her or something.'

'To wring my neck,' interrupted Griselda.

'Well, to hang you or to wring your neck—it comes to the same thing! I threatened to give 'em a thrashing.'

'Harry says you and Tom'll have to fight properly with swords father's got,'

went on Griselda; while the two girls
looked wonderingly at this curious out-
spoken and fearless young person, and
Lady Romayne compressed her lips and
looked unutterable things.

'What a warlike personage!' said Sir
Hubert, amused. 'It ought to suit you,
Hal. But, Withers'—to the tutor—'you'll
have to see they play fair.'

'Harry says he's got to see they p'ay
fair,' said Griselda. But Lady Romayne
told her that little girls ought to be seen
and not heard. She could not prevent Hal
from taking Griselda about the gardens
afterwards, showing her the horses and
dogs, and getting her strawberries and
peaches from the hothouses. But she
determined to do better, in her human
short-sightedness, for, if she could have
foreseen the future, she would have almost

rather have broken the children's acquaintance roughly—cruelly, if need be.
She resolved to do what she could to
make Griselda a fit companion for her
children. No sooner was this good
resolution formed than she began to put
it into practice.

'Hubert, we must really try to reclaim
that little heathen,' she said to her
husband, after Griselda had driven off
home with the escort of the nursemaid
Mary, laden with fruit and flowers for
her mother, ordered by Hal.

'My dear, she is a most amusing little
creature, I am sure,' said the good-natured
baronet.

'She has a soul to be saved.'

'Well, I really think Black is the person
to see to that,' said Sir Hubert.

'He looks so far abroad in that parish

of his, he is always worrying one about
that he doesn't see what is going on
just under his very nose,' said Lady
Romayne severely. 'I am sure that
household must be something quite
shocking, with the wife an invalid, and
no one to look after it.' Then she proposed her really kind idea—to offer Mr
Black teaching from her own governess
for Griselda two or three times weekly.

'I should send Miss Long over to
Crowsfoot in the waggonette, and pay
her something extra,' she added.

'My dear, would it not be much simpler
to have the child here?' suggested Sir
Hubert.

Lady Romayne could not hear of that,
she said, till the child was 'less of a
savage.' So she had an interview in the
schoolroom with the meek Miss Long,

who was always ready to further her patroness's views, and a day or two later she wrote to the Vicar of Crowsfoot,—

'DEAR MR BLACK,—You must excuse my writing to you on a somewhat delicate subject; but, as a mother, who naturally feels and sees matters connected with children which would escape the notice of any man, however well-intentioned, I feel it my duty to do so.

'It really grieved me to see so nice a child as your little daughter so absolutely neglected and entirely wild; and I felt it my duty, in her temporarily motherless condition, to consider what could be done for her. A plan occurred to me to lend you my governess, Miss Long, for some hours each week. We will send her to you, and the carriage can be put up at the

'Lion' while the lessons are given. With kind wishes,—Yours sincerely,

'GERTRUDE ROMAYNE.'

Now Lady Romayne wrote that letter in all good faith—in fact, with a tinge of the noble satisfied feeling she had when sending a large donation to a missionary fund, or putting herself out by lending her handsome drawing-room in town for some meeting connected with the conversion of the heathen.

If she could have seen John Black, and could have known his feelings when he received it, she would have been aghast. It is true that the letter arrived, as such letters frequently will, at the most inopportune moment—on the very morning of the day when the great London physician, Sir Geoffrey Boole, was to visit Crowsfoot

Vicarage and consult with Doctor Mayne on the state of health of the Vicar's dear wife.

John Black had passed a sleepless night, and Mrs Black was much worse.

Two or three times during that warm starlit spring night, when the plants seemed poised in sleep in the genial darkened atmosphere, and the air that came in through the open windows was laden with the heavy perfume of the flowers in the garden-beds and the chestnut-blooms in the fields, a yellow waxen pallor had spread itself upon Evelyn's calm restful face, and she had given that sigh—a mixture of moan and sob—which the Vicar had so often heard coming from dying lips.

How could he sleep? He sat watching her, growing more miserable, more hopeless, each minute. Then in the morning,

after he and Jemima had succeeded in
rallying her from the faintness that en-
sued upon her awakening, and those
sweet blue eyes had looked fondly into
his once more, he went, staggering with
mental and physical exhaustion, into his
study, to find that letter.

It seemed an aggravated insult to the
unhappy man then, there, at that moment.
He just read it through, and, letting it
drop from his hand upon the floor, he
leant his tired head upon his arms with a
stifled sob.

'From the very first that child has been
our curse!' he thought of poor helpless
little Griselda. Poor little maiden, born
in the snow, born into the coldest of the
cold moods of the changeful world!

Then came a sweet little voice at his
elbow, 'Papa, I have brought your coffee!'

and, looking up, there stood Griselda holding a little tray with a cup of steaming, fragrant coffee, and with a world of love and sympathy in her tearful eyes. For, baby that she was, she knew what Jemima's abrupt 'much worse,' when speaking of her mother, meant; and her poor little heart seemed to hurt her at every throb— she felt so very sad.

Her dear, beautiful mother—and that father, who seemed to Griselda so great and noble and grand that her young mind did not place him among men at all—if she could have been interrogated, it would have been found that she ranked him above and beyond 'every one in the world'—her own little expression.

If he had seemed stern the other day, his expression this morning was severity itself.

He took the cup and put it aside without a word. Then he questioned her
closely, bitterly. What had she done—
what had she said, that day at Feather's
Court, to bring about this, which he inwardly called 'that woman's insolence.'

He gathered nothing from Griselda's
replies. Many a child not yet six years
old would have been frightened into in-
coherent acknowledgments, into sobs and
tears. But Griselda stood opposite her
father, firm, composed, only a deep grief
in those wonderful eyes which looked
straight into his.

In any but this hard, wild mood, brought
about by mental torture, that look of silent
reproach would have gone straight to his
heart. As it was, it maddened him. He
felt suddenly that he had better be out
and away ; if he stayed much longer here,

in his suspense and misery, he might be betrayed into some words or actions he would repent.

Looking at his watch, he saw that, if he walked to the station, a mile and a half distant, he would be just in time to meet Sir Geoffrey Boole.

Doctor Mayne was to meet the great man and to drive him to Crowsfoot Vicarage. But the vicar felt that it would be quite as well to be there himself.

He rose abruptly and left Griselda.

The child stood there cold, miserable, suffocated with a new emotion she did not understand. Then she crept away upstairs to her mother's room.

Here it seemed so different,—so peaceful!

Mrs Black, white as one of the
June lilies whose green buds were
beginning to swell upon their tall
stems in the garden below, lay in
her bed. Jemima had 'tidied' the
pretty room, which was always fresh
and neat, with its white dimity hang-
ings. Some bird was singing on a
tree outside. The invalid was drifting
into a drowsy, dreamy content. She
just unclosed her eyes, smiled at her
fair-haired little child, and made a
weak gesture which Griselda knew
meant that she should come and
lie down near her mother, as she
had so often lain before.

She clambered upon the bed, and
creeping close to the still form, nestled
against it. She had learned not to
talk while mother 'was resting.' So

she lay quietly there, feeling an indescribable comfort from her nearness to her gentle, loving mother.

Then Mrs Black, dimly feeling some thought arise in her gradually clouding mind, groped mentally among the soft calming shadows, and half unconsciously spoke it.

'Darling—Griselda,' she dreamily said. 'Tell — Hal — little Hal Romayne — to remember—his promise.'

Then her eyelids drooped; she ebbed slowly—deliciously onward—towards the peace, the rest—where no human thought, no human word, can reach. Griselda's 'Yes, mamma,' seemed floating about somewhere. But she had ridded herself of that last fragment of earthly thought.

And Griselda fell asleep also.

CHAPTER V.

THE vicar found Doctor Mayne talking to the station-master on the empty, breezy platform.

'Hullo! you here?' said the doctor, to whom this was a field day. Deeply sorry as he was for the Blacks, he could not help feeling excited, even elated, at the prospect of a consultation with the great Sir Geoffrey. 'Well, old man, it's a lucky thing I brought the four-wheeler! If I hadn't listened to Mrs Mayne, who was in a consternation at the idea of Sir Geoffrey being fetched in a gig, you'd have had to foot it back through the fields. What's that — train signalled? By Jove, it is! Here she comes!

The little black serpent was winding round a corner, heralded by the puffing white steam. There was a bell-ringing and a general excitement Two or three men in smock - frocks, with bundles, stood by, open - eyed and open - mouthed, as the station-master, whose brisk eye had caught sight of a portly male passenger in one of the two first-class compartments, rushed full tilt at the door and opened it.

'How are ye, doctor—Doctor Mann, did ye say? How are ye?'

The great physician descended affably, if a trifle wearily, from the stuffy carriage where he had spent a couple of hours reading, and wondering why respectable clergymen's wives couldn't contrive to have these desperate illnesses nearer town. Sir Geoffrey was one of those distinguished and prominent personages who can afford to be amiable on all occasions.

Small talk, and much obsequious attention on the part of the station-master and Doctor Mayne, and the doctor's mare was trotting briskly towards Crowsfoot, the doctor driving her, Sir Geoffrey seated on his left, and the Vicar trying to crouch himself in the back seat by almost doubling up his long legs.

'What a pretty little place!' conde-

scendingly observed the great man as
he alighted at the Vicarage door. 'Ah,
my dear sir' — to the vicar — 'you
country clergymen do not half appre-
ciate your surroundings. How you
can study here!'

'How you can die — slowly — here,
rather,' said John Black, almost fiercely.
At which Doctor Mayne gave Sir
Geoffrey a respectful but significant
look; and the authority on the subject
of disease glanced critically at the Vicar,
who in his eyes had suddenly become a patient—a subject—therefore an
entity.

'I will go up and prepare her for
your visit,' said John uneasily, after
he had conducted Sir Geoffrey into
the 'parlour,' which, till so very lately,
had been Evelyn's sitting-room. 'She

has no idea of any danger — has no idea that I asked you to see her.'

'Break it to her gently, my dear sir, but quite as a matter of course,' said Sir Geoffrey, who had assumed his spectacles, and was, as it were, 'in full uniform.' 'Be as short and as practical as possible.'

The Vicar went upstairs. He opened his darling's door with slow, cautious nicety. Then he paused; she was evidently asleep, with Griselda held close to her breast. The two faces were sweet, pale, peaceful, and strangely alike. As he stood there, gazing at the mother who had gathered her child so closely to her heart before she fell asleep, a sudden reproach smote him. He had dared almost to hate that daughter of his whose birth had brought about her mother's suffering; and there, now, he saw and realised that this child was very bone of his beloved wife's bone, flesh of her flesh.

He turned, struck by remorse, and went softly downstairs.

'She—and Griselda—are both asleep,' he said, with a pitiful, appealing glance at Sir Geoffrey.

After some discussion, it was agreed that Sir Geoffrey and Doctor Mayne should visit their patient while in this pleasant slumber.

'When she wakes, the sight of me will make it all right,' confidently said Doctor Mayne. Then, as they went upstairs, he and his superior, he told Sir Geoffrey that this was quite the best thing that could have happened.

'She is intensely nervous,' he said;
'and he is wound up, through his
anxiety, to such a pitch, that the more
he is kept out of it all the better.'

He turned the handle softly. There
lay the two, the sleeping mother and
the sleeping child.

'Asleep?'

Sir Geoffrey said that one word.
Then he looked at Doctor Mayne, and
Doctor Mayne at him.

Yes, asleep—asleep!

John Black waited impatiently below.
How slow they were—how quiet! The
moments seemed hours to his racked
mind. Then he heard ponderous footsteps cross the floor above, and come
down the stairs cautiously, heavily.
One of them coming down to fetch
him — or what? He started to his

feet as Doctor Mayne came into the
room, carrying Griselda, asleep.

The doctor's ruddy face was dis-
composed. His colour came and went
unhealthily. His voice was hoarse, and
trembled as he said,—

'You must bear up, my friend.'

Then he sat down and called his
attention to the pale little child. 'She
is not strong,' he said; 'poor little
darling; your wife's legacy to you!'

Then he turned away his head,
dreading to see the effect of his words.
He knew this old, oft-repeated scene
in life's drama so far too well. Some
would fall down, shrieking. Others
would curse and rave, and afterwards
would not guess how they had blas-
phemed Death, the thief who had
robbed them of their treasures. As

a rule, the weak women bore their blows the best, because they had not the instinct to fight and evade them, and a mental shock knocked them down and disabled them at once.

'She is dead?' said John Black, with perfect composure.

The doctor looked round in fear. But the Vicar, though pale with an ugly leaden pallor, seemed to hear his 'Yes' followed by the assurance that her precious soul must have fled— quietly, peacefully, as a bird starts on its homeward flight—as if it were some ordinary acquiescence.

'I will go upstairs; you had better come too,' he said. Then he took a cushion from a chair, arranged it upon Mrs Black's sofa, and, taking the sleeping child from Doctor Mayne with minute care, placed her there, and covered her with the knitted rug which had so often covered her dead mother.

Then he led the way, and joined Sir Geoffrey, who was awaiting him, and who greeted him with genuine sympathy. Looking at that pale, dead beauty, the celebrated physician had felt that this man's loss was great indeed.

Both doctors, by a common human instinct, walked away and conversed in whispers at the window, while John Black took his first look at his wife— in death.

What he felt—what he thought, as he kissed the half-opened eyelids close upon those lovely eyes, which would never gaze into his with deep, confid-

ing love again—was no one's—no human
being's right to know. It was not
long before he joined the two doctors,
and, inviting them to remain for a
while in the parlour—Evelyn's parlour
—went to break the news to Jemima
and to the boys.

.   .   .   .

'I like to see pluck,' said Sir Geoffrey, as Doctor Mayne was driving
him back to the station an hour afterwards. 'I like to see character. Now,
there was character in the way that
man took his loss. He is a fellow with
a great deal in him, and, under favour-
able circumstances, should make his
mark in the world.'

But the little Crowsfoot doctor —
who, although he had not written
scientific works, or had 'made his

name,' had a natural shrewd insight into human nature born of much practice—shook his head.

'You don't know John Black,' he said. Then he told Sir Geoffrey all he himself knew of the Vicar's peculiar position in life. 'Now, if he had stormed and raved—if his brain had given way—I should be full of hope for him. But he is too strong, that is the fact—too strong. He fights fate; and when once a man begins to do that —well, he is no longer fit to help his fellow-creatures, for it will take all his time, and all his energy, and all his spirit, and in the long run he must be worsted.'

'True,' said Sir Geoffrey. 'But I should hope that that very beautiful little girl would be a softening influence in his life.'

'Let us hope so,' said Doctor Mayne doubtfully. 'But, in my poor opinion, we may be said to have lost our genial, whole-hearted Vicar. The John Black I have walked hand - in - hand with—who has been, as it were, a living storehouse of help, and sympathy, and counsel, and strength—will be buried in his wife's grave. The man I have seen to-day — well, I would rather not think of what that man, with his brain-power, in his position, might become.'

.   .   .   .

It was a pleasant, drowsy summer after-noon. Hot sunshine was tempered by a fresh breeze, that swayed the leafy boughs in the churchyard, and, waving the long grass upon the green graves, made the sturdy ivy-leaves that clung to the head-stones or railings shiver and tremble.

Crowsfoot Church, the grey - stone edifice which the Vicar had changed from a tumble-down, whitewash-smeared building into a comely little place of prayer, stood on a slope above the Vicarage — above the village. The graves that lay in rows about the churchyard were fanned by summer winds and beaten upon by winter storms.

The turf laid on Mrs Black's grave was green, after the rain of many days. The wreaths and nosegays sent by sympathising parishioners—whose hearts were full of gratitude to John Black, their constant friend, as well as their hard-working pastor — had been beaten into masses of light-brown pulp, and had been swept off, and cast upon a growing heap of dead leaves in the churchyard corner by the sexton.

The grave was close to the path. Mrs Black, who had loved life and the living, had once said to her husband in their early marriage days, 'If I die before you, John, don't have me put away in a damp corner, where no one goes; at least, let me feel the tread of footsteps, and hear human voices.'

And in the midst of his stony dry-eyed anguish—smiling a grim smile of unbelief in the idea that the soulless, senseless clay could know or feel—the Vicar remembered his wife's curious fancy, and chose her grave where the villagers must pass each Sunday as they went to church.

The first Sunday there were little groups of silent mourners. He saw them — once more smiling that crude, repellent smile. 'I gave them two or three Sundays at the utmost,' he said to himself. On the fourth Sunday he looked out from the vestry window. He watched them go down that path in twos or threes. He saw them pass the grave. Some went carelessly by; a few cast a cursory glance that way. One or two only stayed a second, making some remark, then walked hastily on. He did not blame them; but his heart was hardening. He went that night by moonlight to the place where the cold body that had contained the spirit he had loved lay hidden away. He tried to feel that Evelyn, or part of what had been Evelyn, was there. He could not. He went home, feeling more petrified than ever.

Others felt the change in him also.

A worthy young couple in the village
lost their only child—a bright, vigorous
little lad. He died of rapid convulsions
in his mother's arms. Formerly the
Vicar would have been overflowing with
sympathy. Now he strode in, and
whatever he found to say aggravated
the grief of the bereaved parents. He
had no gentle reminders of the beautiful
death-tales in the Gospel to give. He
did not talk of the slightness and short-
ness of life till the aching hearts of the
mourners were solaced, as he used to
do. He told a few harsh truths—that
these things were—therefore they must
be accepted. 'It was hard to kick
against the pricks,' and the sooner they
stifled their grief, and found comfort in
active life and forgetfulness, the better
for them.

The poor young parents looked blankly at one another after he had gone. Then the young mother flung herself into her husband's arms, and, in weeping out her heart's grief in his arms, those sceptical hard sayings flew harmlessly over her poor little head— brainless, perhaps, but a sound auxiliary in her honest, every-day life.

Meanwhile, Evelyn Black's chief mourner was the little daughter who had lain on her breast when she gave back her sweet life to Heaven.

Griselda had kissed her mother's coffin. She had watched it carried out of the house under the silk and velvet pall, her father, Tom, and Harry, following. She had sat watching while Jemima, with swollen eyes and heaving chest, had arranged her mother's room to look as

little like it was wont to look as possible. Then, feeling as if home were
removed to the churchyard, as it were,
she had stolen off to her mother's grave.

That earth-mound was not to her the
mere mound of earth it was to others.
The very first time she saw it, it seemed
familiar and natural. When she crouched
by it, and clasped the rough lumps of
clay with her little arms, she was comforted. Perhaps her dear mother had
never seemed so much her own mother
as she did buried down there and left
all alone.

'Mother, dear,' she whispered, her soft
lips close to the holes in the earth, 'I
am here — Griselda.' Then she would
stick a row of flowers from the Vicarage
garden along the head of the grave, and
water them with water she brought in

the little green watering-can her mother gave her on her last birthday.

On this bright June afternoon she had stolen out ; she had brought two little pots of musk the old gardener had given her, and had nestled them against the grave. Then she sat crouched up near to them, sheltered from the wind by a tall head-stone close by, and began to knit a garter for Harry, whose stockings were always coming down.

'You and I'll have to be mother to those boys now ; it'll be all the mother they're likely to get,' Jemima had said to Griselda, soon after her mistress's death. And Griselda had thought a good deal about that already. She pitied ' the boys,' and ran about to fetch things for them, and put her jam on Harry's plate when he was not looking, and stole up-

stairs and picked up Tom's clothes, which
he had a trick of flinging about the room,
to save him a scolding from Jemima. She
never once thought that it was she herself who had suffered the greatest loss.

As for her father, she had hardly dared
think of him, much less look at or speak
to the gaunt haggard man who crept in
and out of the house like a black shadow
of his former self.

She only thought of him here—at the
grave. She longed to be grown up, a
woman—to talk to her father and make
him laugh, as her mother used to do.
It was not to be expected that a little
child like she was could be anything but
a trouble.

She was thinking hard, her baby lips
pressed close together, her earnest eyes
riveted on the knitting her unaccustomed

fingers were struggling with, when Hal
Romayne came along the path towards
her.

He had ridden over twice since Mrs
Black's death — the first time with in-
quiries, when Jemima, who had found
out something about that inopportune
letter of Lady Romayne's, only half
opened the street door, and sent him off
as quickly as possible ; the second time
with a letter of condolence, one day when
Griselda happened to be spending the
day with Mrs Mayne, the doctor's wife.

To-day he had dressed in black out
of compliment to Griselda, and looked
slightly awe-stricken as he went to seek
his little friend at her mother's grave,
according to Jemima's recommendation.
Death had not been brought before him
until now ; and he had a lively remem-

brance of the beautiful woman on the
sofa in the Vicarage parlour, who talked
to him with such winning seriousness.

They had a French picture, *Les Deux
Orphelines*, in one of the drawing-rooms
at Feather's Court, and he had unconsciously expected to see Griselda
with her tearful eyes lifted to the sky,
after the manner of those dismal little
beings. So that when Griselda, hearing a footstep, looked up, dropped her
work, and ran to meet him with a joy-
ous ' Oh, Hal ! ' he felt decidedly relieved, although he tacitly resisted when
she pulled him towards the grave, and
he suggested going back to the Vicarage.

' But you must come to the grave,'
she insisted. ' Besides, mother told me
to tell you something.'

' But she is not there,' said Hal, looking askance at the mound. 'Don't you know she is far away—in heaven?'

'Heaven is not far away,' said Griselda decidedly. 'It is just over the tops of the trees, that's all.'

'Not the heaven where the angels are,' said Hal; 'that is ever so far off.'

'There are not two heavens,' said Griselda. 'And up there, where the birds fly and the larks go up singing, isn't earth, so it must be heaven.'

'But—' began Hal. Then he forgot what he meant to say—in fact, he was somewhat puzzled how to teach Griselda that her notions were wrong, so he went on, 'What was it your mother said about me?'

'It was just before she went to sleep for good,' said Griselda, kneeling down, her little hand laid protectingly upon the

grave, and her great violet eyes lit up
by the recollection. 'She said, " Tell
Hal Romayne to remember his promise."'

Hal was but a young boy, and he was
sensitive. This message from the grave,
as it seemed to him, was unnerving.
For a moment he was scared — what
promise — when — how — where made,
and to whom ? Then suddenly it all
came back to him—the day he went first
to the Vicarage, his visit to the orchard,
Griselda's introduction of him to her
mother, and her pleading voice as she
confided little Griselda to his care. He
had promised the dead woman who lay
in that grave to take care of her child ;
and in boyish impetuosity he said to
himself, ' And they may say what they
like, but I'll do it too.'

He looked down at the fair little creature, who was wonderingly watching the changing, varied expressions as they flitted across 'her prince's' handsome face, with a new interest and tenderness. She belonged to him in some way, not yet defined; he had pledged his word that she should do so.

'Griselda,' he said, forgetting his awe of graves and the dead in this new solemnity, and kneeling down beside her, 'do you know I came to-day to tell you that I am going away—I am going to school?'

'Oh, dear!' said Griselda, distressed. 'And I thought you would come again —very soon.'

'So I will, in the holidays,' said Hal. Then he told her how he must go to school, to learn to be a man. 'You can't spend all your days with girls and

women, you know,' he added, with a
tinge of disdain when alluding to her
sex, which impressed Griselda more
than any words would have done with
the supremacy and glory of manhood.
' If I grew up a molly-coddle, I shouldn't
be fit to take care of you. And I am
going to.'

He rose and drew a long breath.
Griselda gazed up at him with round,
admiring eyes. He looked a handsome
lad, with his curly head thrown back ;
so slim and straight, too, in his black
velvet suit.

' I shall marry you when I grow up,'
he said, with a feeling that he had to
take a plunge, and the sooner it was
over the better. ' What do you think
of that ? '

Griselda shook her head.

'They wouldn't let you,' she replied. 'Besides, if they did, I couldn't leave father.'

'Oh, I shall be able to look after him!' said Hal, with a spice of contempt. Lady Romayne had not inveighed against Mr Black's culpable neglect of his children, within earshot of her precocious son, without effect.

'Would you marry him too?' asked Griselda, to whom marriage was another word for home and companionship.

'I can't tell what I shall do. It is such a long time off,' said Hal loftily. 'I shouldn't have told you I meant to marry you, only I thought it might be something for you to look forward to, if · those boys are rude, or you feel lonely, or anything.'

He knelt down again, and took her

little hand. She was looking serious,
half-pleased, half-doubtful. If she had
appeared overwhelmed by Hal's magnificent statement, he would not have
liked her half so much as he did at
that moment, when he found that this
simple, almost rustic, little maiden was
not so easily dazzled and surprised out
of the even tenor of her way, although
she admired him, he knew, as much as,
if not more than, she had ever admired
anything throughout her little life.

'You must give me something to
keep,' he said—'something of yours.'

'I haven't anything,' she said. She
was dressed in a plain black frock, and
in an old white pinafore. She wore the
same blue sun-bonnet as when he first
saw her. It was not mourning, but
Jemima had not thought well to ask

her master for money to buy another.
'I haven't anything, really,' she repeated earnestly.   Then she remembered her little silver locket which
Jemima kept in a top drawer in her
room.   But Hal would not take this
solitary jewel of his lady-love's.   He
would have a spray of musk.   He took
out his russia-leather purse, and she
dropped the tiny green sprig with the
yellow flower into one of its many
compartments.

'Now I must give you something,'
he said, as he replaced the purse in his
breast-pocket.   'It wouldn't be fair to
the governor to give you my watch;
he had my monogram put upon it in
diamonds'—taking out his watch, and
showing the glittering case to the astonished Griselda.   'You can't have the

seal either—it's a signet—but you can
have this.'

He detached the seal and watch from
his chain, and tossed the gold cable into
her lap.

She did not want to take it. She
was distressed. But he insisted, and
she allowed him to take her home to
the Vicarage, holding her promise that
she would not show that watch-chain
to anyone—not even to Jemima.

'If you do, there'll be the deuce and
all to pay,' he assured her — a threat
which made her tremble, for, in her
ignorance of 'the deuce and all,' she
imagined a crew of hobgoblins pursuing
and haunting her for this undefined but
evidently terrible reckoning.

'I won't,' she assured him sturdily, just
as they came in sight of the Feather's

Court groom walking Hal's new roan pony up and down. 'But you'll come in ?'

'No,' said Hal, with a qualm of conscience, although he was firmly persuaded of his own rectitude, if not generosity. 'No; I don't think I will —to-day.'

Then he asked her to write to him from time to time. But she could only print a little bit, and that would scarcely do. He suggested Jemima for a scribe. But, according to Griselda, Jemima could only 'make crosses.'

'Never mind; I know what to do,' were Hal's final words, as, carefully refraining from the kiss which on a former occasion had cost him much chagrin, he mounted his pony; and he rode straight away to Doctor Mayne's house, at the further end of the village.

'Can I see Mrs Mayne, if you please?' he asked of the buxom house-maid who appeared in answer to his ring.

'I will see, sir,' she said, reddening as she recognised 'little Master Romayne.' And she sped away, returning almost immediately to say, 'Would you walk this way, if you please, sir?'

Hal was ushered into the doctor's dining-room, which was all red and mahogany, with a faint odour of old sherry and fruit and jessamine—there was a climbing jessamine just outside, where Mrs Mayne sat at work, piles of fair, white linen on the table, on the sofa—everywhere.

'How do you do, Master Romayne?' Plump, comely, little Mrs Mayne was just a trifle flattered by this unexpected visit. 'I hope your dear mamma and papa are quite well?'

Hal assured her that they were, with a preternatural gravity which he considered appropriate to the occasion.

'I have not come on account of the family, Mrs Mayne,' he said, 'with the grandeur of a young Hamlet,' as Mrs Mayne afterwards described him. 'I have come to you as the friend of poor Mrs Black.'

'Oh, of course, certainly!' said Mrs Mayne, almost as much surprised by this mature talk from the young heir of Feather's Court as if her favourite tabby, who was blinking at her from the white wool hearthrug, had suddenly found human speech. 'But do have some cake, Master Romayne, or a glass of home-made wine.' Mrs Mayne hesi-

tated to offer such a boy claret or
sherry.

'I thank you; no,' replied Hal, copy-
ing the manner of a well-known dean,
lately a visitor at the Court. 'I do
not eat between meals; I thank you!
No, Mrs Mayne; the truth is—can I
really trust you?' he went on, with a
sudden change to the manner of an
eager boy. Then, upon Mrs Mayne's
earnest assurance that he could, he told
his story—how he had made Mrs Black
a promise to look after Griselda, and
how she had sent him a reminder
from her death-bed.

'And now I am going away to
school,' he went on; 'and I want to
know how she gets on. She can't
write, you know, and she says that servant of theirs can only make crosses,

so I thought perhaps you would write to me now and then.'

Mrs Mayne, although somewhat startled by this very 'grown-up' little boy's talk, undertook to do what she could in the matter.

It was only after Hal had ridden off, solemnly saluting her, that she began to realise what this meant.

'It was so strange, my dear, a boy talking like that, that I forgot it would be scarcely right to the parents, and that I really ought not to do anything of the sort,' she assured her husband later on.

'My dear, the parents would only laugh,' said her good-natured spouse, who was hugely amused. 'I don't mean poor Black; there doesn't seem to be a laugh left in him. But the Romaynes

—why, they know they can afford to give their son rope. Some years hence he will have forgotten that poor little maid.'

'Not he!' said Mrs Mayne warmly. 'There's a good deal more in that lad than you give him credit for, Thomas.'

'Ah, well, I shall never be astonished at anything that happens to that poor little mite Griselda!' said the doctor. 'If I were superstitious, I should have all sorts of strange notions about her. She has been the innocent cause of her mother's death; the innocent cause of poor Black's wreck—for it is nothing more nor less than a moral wreck—any fool can see that. What is there surprising, after this, that she should bewitch a boy, and make him behave in that curious way? Nothing could be stranger than her birth—nothing; and I have heard and read that as people are born so they go on through life, and so they die; and, small though my own poor personal experience is, it points to the truth of that.'

Mrs Mayne sighed.

'Poor child!' she said. 'I believe that unlucky incident of being born in the snow, in that barn, will stick to her through life, and perhaps spoil it.'

'It might, only there happens to be such a thing as Providence,' said the doctor dryly.

CHAPTER VI.

IT was ten years later; early autumn in a German cathedral city. The broad Rhine flowed between the busy towns—for the city was divided, and linked by a curious bridge of boats. The great tower of the unfinished cathedral rose high above the masses of quaint houses. It came upon you as a surprise, a monster edifice decorated with scaffolding, as you turned some corner, after losing yourself in a maze of narrow, winding streets. Hal Romayne, now a slight, handsome young

man, about to come of age, was passing through on his way to Switzerland
with Sir Hubert, Lady Romayne, and his
sisters.   It was 'the girls'' first trip.
Hal had been abroad twice before ; his
third visit bored him.   He could not
understand how Mabel, the brighter of
the two girls, could 'gush' over everything — from the churches with their
tawdry chapels, to the old market-
women with their quaint caps and great
earrings, shouting and chattering amid
their piles of purple plums and yellow
apricots or green cabbages, under their
gay umbrellas.   The noise and clatter
tired him.   This morning he had left
'the girls,' meekly attended by Sir
Hubert, whom they 'managed'—as the
languid Lydia termed their subjection
of their good-natured father — buying

rosaries, pictures, medals, as mementos, and had returned to the hotel to 'moon about' by himself. Lady Romayne had gone for a drive. The courier was bustling about, fussing over the arrangements for their further journeying. Hal felt the first symptoms of one of those fits of *ennui* which he dreaded, and which nothing would cure, because they arose from overdoing the thing called Pleasure — in fact, from satiety. He threw open his window and leaned out. Sailors were shouting as the slim-masted crafts heaved on the river waves. Men swarmed up and down the vessels' sides, loading; trollies were noisily clattering about the rough stones of the wharves. Then the steamer came puffing in, and tourists, mostly English in their eternal tweed suits and veiled hats and serge costumes, came herding hastily upon shore, rushing and crushing as they would scarcely have cared to do at home, followed by bloused porters shouldering luggage.

It was vulgar. 'Those British tourists are like a plague of locusts over the face of the globe,' Hal disgustedly told himself. Then he ill-temperedly seized his hat and hurried out.

The narrow, untidy streets were quiet now, in this city where the natives rose at sunrise and went to bed while it was still day. Wandering aimlessly, he came upon the very side-door of the cathedral where he had left his father and sisters an hour or two ago. But the spot was deserted; the market was over. Only the refuse scattered about the stones, and a pile of empty baskets in a corner,

remained of this morning's busy scene.
An old dog lay wearily under a little
image in a niche, as if he had sheltered
there from his tormentors, the boys.
As Hal came towards him, he half
opened his tired eyes and limped away.
There was a great sore on his lame
leg. Hal felt a choke in his throat at
the sight of the forlorn, ill-used creature.
He stooped and patted him, with kind
words. He felt he would have given
treble its price for a piece of meat for
that homeless mongrel who looked up
so abjectly into his face. At that moment a sad chant arose in the church,—

' *Agnus Dei, qui tollis peccata mundi, miserere.*'

It was the choir rehearsing a requiem
mass which was to be given to-morrow
—the requiem of a good priest who died
of malignant fever, caught from a sick

person to whom he had ministered. The chant came floating out. Hal felt curiously wretched, alone, as a Pariah among his kind, who cared little for him, as he cared little for them.

He held a commission in a 'swell' regiment. He had gone into the army full of military enthusiasm, to find that to seek to study the science of war was considered 'bad form,' and that the only officers who deserved the name were one or two conceited martinets, who, being detested and scorned, did more harm than good.

He would have embraced his profession with ardour; but he found it a mere shadow. There was no substance to embrace. Parade, drill, mess — this was the life. The more dissipated and reckless a fellow was, the more popular.

There was nothing between a watery
atheism and a fanatic sectarianism, which
was so Pharisaical that blasphemy seemed
sounder and more honest. In his own
words, he 'felt as if he had been flung
upon a dunghill,' an exaggerated sensation, which Lady Romayne exerted whatever influence she possessed to combat.

'Because, my dear,' she said to her
husband in private, 'Hal is so impetuous and excitable that he really must
have an occupation. Now, there are only
three professions for us unfortunates —
the bar, the church, and the army. Hal
has no taste for the law. There are
such riff-raff in the church now—that it
ranks very low in my estimation. But
while commissions are to be bought, and
they keep up the mess, we shall at least
have officers who are public-school men.'

So Hal Romayne attended his sovereign's *levée* as a commissioned officer, and, as heir to an old as well as a rich baronetcy, was so pestered with invitations to dinners, balls, and society entertainments of every description, that, in his own words, 'one season sickened him of the lot.'

Yes, that promised to be his bane in life—his capacity to be easily sickened. He found the verb 'to loathe' far easier to conjugate than the verb 'to love.' Yet here he was nearer a feeling of love than he had been for years, and that love for a poor ugly, wounded old dog.

He longed—he could not tell why or wherefore — to take that poor canine cripple tenderly in his arms, and carry it into the church. He stood looking at the dog, and listening to that lovely, mournful music. The tired animal's head had drooped upon its paws, and it had dozed off. Sleep—death—these were the highest blessings for creatures such as this. He wanted to hear that music nearer. 'And the poor beast won't move,' he thought. So he went into the old porch, past the grim sculptured saints and martyrs who seemed to grow out of the stone looking heavenward with folded hands,—and, pushing open the heavy carved oaken door, found himself in the church — from the hot glare into cool, pleasant shade. At first sight, the great grey interior seemed deserted. The shadows came and went high up above among the lofty arches. The mournful chanting rose, fell, and echoed. There were

two or three figures flitting about beyond the great screen, near to the high
altar. He stood, hat in hand, for a
few minutes, thinking strange thoughts
of life and death. Such a dissatisfied,
restless nature as his was not super-
ficial. His continual discontent led to
mental inquiry, then to thought. There
had been some strong impressions made
upon him in his boyhood. One of
these was his acquaintance with the
dying Mrs Black. He remembered
that episode in his young life as little
as he would remember a scar. But,
like a scar-producing wound, it had left
its mark.

He had neither forgotten nor neglected
Griselda all these years; but chance, or
fate—largely assisted by Lady Romayne
—had ordained that they should meet

but seldom. In the summer holidays
the Romaynes went to the coast for
sea - bathing. Christmas they generally
spent with General Sir Joseph Manton,
Lady Romayne's father, at his old-
fashioned Welsh retreat. Since Mrs
Black's death, Hal had met Griselda
about a dozen times.

He was not one to dream and ponder
over past sensations. So, although he
thought kindly, even tenderly, of the
little maiden he had determined, when
he was a boy, to marry some day,
Griselda was an exception in his life.
She had never been farther from his
thoughts than to-day, when, wandering
into a chapel to see an old Italian picture—a *Mater Dolorosa* that had made
an impression upon him the first time
he visited the cathedral a year or two

ago—he suddenly came upon Griselda herself.

Two old market-women were kneeling, bowing, and muttering, their rosaries in their hands. Griselda was standing, bending — her arms resting upon the balustrade of the altar-rails—gazing into the picture he had come to see.

It was unmistakably Griselda. She was dressed in a cotton gown, with no attempt at fashion in its make ; but even her little straw hat could not hide that golden glory of hair, or the shape of her perfect little head.

CHAPTER VII.

A S Hal Romayne recognised Griselda, with her hands resting on the altar-rails of the little chapel—the pretty fair profile with the short upper lip and softly-rounded chin dark against a stray sun-ray which was peeping in—he felt a certain shock. This meeting here like this, so unexpected, seemed to him to have something uncanny in it. Then, when the beautiful young girl turned her head, and, at once recognising him, merely smiled, he felt as if this were more uncanny still.

'Did you know we were here?' were the first words he spoke to her, in the hushed voice of one whose respect for the house of God is not yet dead, as they touched each other's hands ceremoniously.

'No,' she said.

She was not surprised—not agitated, in fact. Signs of emotion were entirely absent in her, while he was chilled, and trembled.

'You are not alone?' he asked.

'My father is going round with the sacristan,' she said. 'Of course, we have not seen you for so long, you do not know; my father—is—taking pupils.'

'Indeed!' said Hal, wondering at the tone of anguish with which she informed him of an every-day fact.

'Yes,' said Griselda, her fair eyelids

veiling her beautiful eyes, 'my father's voice threatens to give way. He has left off preaching for some time, and perhaps soon he will not be able to read the prayers; so, with this threatening, he has had to engage a curate. This expense has had to be met by his taking pupils.'

'Yes,' said Hal respectfully, himself chivalrous again, once the surprise and its effect over. 'No one could coach better than your father, I am sure; he is dreadfully clever.'

'You have seen the reviews?' said Griselda, suddenly raising those big violet eyes, and fixing them with a strained, anxious expression upon the young man.

'Reviews?' he repeated, with an 'utterly-at-sea' sensation. What could she mean?

'The antagonistic reviews upon his book—*Certain Passages in Holy Writ Examined by a Clergyman of the Church of England,*' said Griselda. The quarterlies were simply scorching. The bishop wrote very kindly, but severely. Surely you have heard all about it?'

Hal shook his head.

'I am afraid we military fellows are so degenerate that we neither read controversial books nor the comments of the quarterlies,' he said, with a short laugh. 'But, Griselda, if this book and pupil business has been a trouble to you, that is another affair altogether.'

Griselda smiled. It was a curious smile to see upon a young fresh face— the smile of one who is asked some absurdity, such as a senior wrangler

just loaded with laurels might give if
a boy asked him if he had ever learnt
rule of three, or a bibliomaniac, if some
one ignorant of his craze asked him if
he was fond of books.

'Trouble to my father, you mean?'
she said. 'I am only a girl. Girls don't
have troubles.'

'No; you are scarcely one to go into
hysterics if a new gown doesn't fit
according to your liking, like Lydia,
or to come home from hunting in a
rage because some other lady got the
brush, like Mabel,' said Hal. 'But,
trouble or no trouble, is your father
ill, or merely knocked over by disap-
pointment?'

'Look at him!' said Griselda; and
there was a hopelessness in her voice.

While speaking, they had strolled out

of the side-chapel into the nave. Hal,
shading his eyes with his hand from a
long sunbeam that fell straight upon the
pavement in front from a side window,
saw three figures coming towards them.
One was the stooping form of the grey-
haired old sacristan, tottering along in his
black gown, his bunch of keys dangling
from one of his withered hands; another
was John Black, thinner, but still holding
up the head which was now sparsely
covered with straggling grey hair. There
was a fierce, determined look on his gaunt
face; you would have judged him to be
a man of will, purpose, strength, who
had been worsted, hunted down by Fate,
and now stood morally at bay. And
such a guess would not have been altogether wrong. The third was a young
man, somewhat squarely, if slightly, built,

with sharp, busy grey eyes in a face which was pleasant, if not handsome. His hair was rough; his summer grey suit hung helplessly upon him; his hands were gloveless, sunburnt—in fact, he looked what he was, a mathematician.

'Is that Hugh Blunt, your father's pupil?' asked Hal, with astonishment and distaste. 'Why, he was reading with my tutor, and was going into the army!'

'Well, he is reading for his "B.S.C." now,' said Griselda. 'He likes my father.'

There was an ineffable tenderness in that sentence, just as there was the very reverse in the nods and 'how are you's?' of the young men when they met.

'I did not know that you two were acquainted,' said the Vicar of Crowsfoot, glancing from one to the other with a certain grim amusement

'We met at Robarts' rooms,' said Hal coolly; the fact being that Blunt—who distanced Romayne in study as a flash of lightning a slow-travelling cloud—had spoken contemptuously of Hal to the mathematical coach, Mr Robarts, as a 'howling swell,' while Hal had languidly wondered to the tutor why it was that, when a fellow was clever, he ceased to comb his hair and brush his nails. 'It only takes five minutes, you know,' Hal had said. 'There is no excuse on the ground of time.' Those two were antagonistic. John Black knew it at a glance. Griselda felt it. An awkwardness came to the four English people so strangely met thus to-day in a foreign cathedral. Their disjointed talk meant nothing. They were adversaries, till they shut the oaken door and went out into the warm air, the gay sunshine, with great heaven as their dome instead of men's carvings in hard, cold stone.

Here Hal remembered the dog, told Griselda about the poor lame cur, and together they went across to the corner where he was dozing, crouched against a buttress.

'Poor, poor creature!' said Griselda. Then her father came up, and was immediately interested. He had not lost pity for humanity's weaknesses in his scorn for humanity's callous selfishness. One of humanity's weaknesses, in his eyes, was its carelessness of animals.

'Another unfortunate victim,' he said; and, turning the timid, wounded creature gently over, he appraised its condition.

'Three-quarters dead of starvation,' was his verdict. 'Stoned, hunted, and frightened, perhaps, into rabies.'

Up came Hugh Blunt, who loved his own retriever at home better than any other living creature, and the four grew friendly in a common sympathy for a low-bred outcast among dogs. Friendly—animated even. They discussed a possible owner, and were unanimous in their decision—none. Then came the problem, what was to be done with him? Solved by Griselda pleading to take him back to their hotel. She would find a home for him. Griselda's adoption of the cur proposed, seconded, and passed, the next question was how to convey him to the hotel. Griselda coaxed him, and he limped painfully into the road, but stood blinking his sore, tearful eyes so piteously

at one after the other, his whole attitude
so expressive of, 'Why torment me ? why
not leave me to die ?' that impetuous Hal,
feeling a rush of pity, simply stooped,
and, lifting the dirty creature. cradled him
in his arms.

'Show me the way,' he said, striding
off. Griselda—hurrying along at his side,
directing him to turn to the left, through
this narrow street, and to bear round to
the right up another—had never admired
Hal Romayne more, not even when he
had suddenly appeared in his green velvet
splendour as her promised prince in the
orchard of Crowsfoot Vicarage.

'Oh, your coat!' she ventured to say.
It seemed to her such a delicate garment,
and already it was getting smeared and
hairy.

'Bother my coat!' said Hal. 'I am

beginning to detest coats. I am sick of the same eternal old pattern. Why don't they invent something new? I don't want to wear a coat. I would wear any mortal thing—for a change.'

Ay, for a change. To Hal change was as welcome as ice to the fever-parched, drink to the thirsty.

It was a change, carrying that old dog through the streets, Griselda, sweet, fresh as a mountain daisy, speeding along eagerly at his side—a change to see the old women stop short and watch the strange procession, arms akimbo on their broad hips, their eyes slight with admiring astonishment; strange to go into the humble inn, ' Die Weisse Rose ' (the white rose), where a rose, like a pictured super-annuated turnip, presided as signboard, where it was all very neat and tidy, but where passages, coffee-room, and staircase were alike pervaded by a strong odour of sauerkraut and roasting coffee, and where the house-mistress and the two red-faced red-armed women her assistants, talked to their guests,—however distinguished those guests might be, and they had had some learned, ay, some great men, with world-wide-known names, here,—with an equality and fraternity which did them honour.

It was all new, thought Hal, as Griselda told the old dog's story in German to the woman with the gigantic flaxen plaits, the blue, blue eyes; her father, Hal, and young Blunt standing by—but newest of all was Griselda herself—so lovely, so pitying, and so supremely unconscious of being anything, anyone, anybody — indeed, an entity at all.

It was very new—to face the great hotel, with its exclusive fashionable air, its 'stand off' grandeur—after this; to arrive just as his mother was alighting—discontentedly, for she had not been amused by her drive—and to hear her fretful 'Dear me! Where have you been? You might have come with me to direct the coachman. He has taken me along the most uninteresting road,' *et cætera.*

'Do you know what I have been doing?' said Hal, with a saucy coolness which he assumed for his women relatives —a coolness which meant that they might kick against his will, they might struggle, resist, upbraid, reproach, weep, shriek, or faint—and he would not 'care a rap.' 'I have been to the cathedral, worshipping a picture—nearer saying my prayers among the old women mumbling over their beads than I have been for months. After which, I carried a mangy old dog right from one end of the town to the other, followed by a select but somewhat ragged crowd of admiring natives; and I ended up by drinking small beer and smoking a clay pipe in a cheap and nasty public-house with a British parson, who has come abroad to pursue his studies in Atheism among the Roman Catholic heathen.'

'Good gracious!' gasped Lady Romayne, with a little start.

'Ah,' said Hal meaningly, 'I see you know all about it! Now, mother, it is shabby--mean of you not to have told me about the Blacks.'

Lady Romayne disgustedly said there was nothing much to tell, only 'that man had turned out just as she had expected—

just like those men who idealise and spoil the uneducated poor always did. They begin by knowing better than their betters, and end by knowing better than their Creator.' Lady Romayne grew quite sarcastic in her annoyance that, after all her plans and precautions to prevent Hal from seeing or knowing anything of the Blacks, they and Hal should actually have met in this untoward and out-of-the-way manner.

'The man got tired of flaunting his Radicalism in people's faces, especially when he got no encouragement from the county people,' she went on ; 'so he wrote a book, a vulgar attack upon the Epistles. It was just what such a man would do. However, his arrogance met with its just reward. The papers put him down with a calm contempt; the bishop gave him a good scolding. He was treated like

a naughty little boy or a silly, snar-
ling puppy. He was cautioned not to
preach—'

'What ?'

'That was the very least the bishop
could do, I am sure,' said Lady Romayne, placidly pursuing her way up
the grand staircase to her private
apartments. 'If it had not been for
the loss of his wife years ago, and
that fuss about it, I am quite sure
the bishop's duty would have been to
suspend him altogether.'

'Defend me from women's spiteful,
venomous tongues !'

'Hal, you forget yourself !'

'I do not forget poor Griselda.'

'Poor Griselda, as you call her,
is, in my opinion, a remarkably silly
young person,' said Lady Romayne,

panting a little as she gained the sitting-room, which was all crimson velvet and gilding, and as she sank among the cushions of the nearest sofa,—'I have always noticed that people who get called "poor" are foolish, useless creatures, from Sterne's imaginary "Maria," who was doubtless drawn from life, down to that lady your grandpapa is so kind to —Lady Gladys Lewis—who weeps at everything that happens to her, good, bad, or indifferent.'

'Mother, you ought to have been a friend to Griselda,' said Hal hotly. He had grown pale, and his dark brows were knit, which meant anger.

Lady Romayne was determined not to lose her temper. Coolness was her only chance with her spoilt boy.

'I am a good friend to Griselda Black,' she said, 'but I cannot approve of her. I am told that she sat up with her father night after night helping him in the concoction of that vile book.'

'You cannot approve of such a glorious thing?'

'You young officers are unfortunately such a set of unbelievers, that I cannot expect you to understand me, Hal! We do not feel surprised when you men go off at a tangent and believe in nothing. We know that, at the very first blow from the Almighty, you will be down grovelling— cowards at heart, as you all are! But a woman is quite a different affair. She must be very bad—or a fool—if she does not believe. So that girl is evidently a fool. I expect her mother was, before her, or the man would not be in this strait.'

' I must not argue with a lady,' said Hal, with a mock bow of respect; then he went off downstairs to the smoking-room, and got a chair near the window, and a *Galignani*, and sat smoking and dreaming of Griselda — Griselda, who looked like some perfect statue come to life and masquerading in a cotton frock—Griselda, who had sat up nights with her father, who dared front the world side by side with him, no matter what his opinions. ' If creatures such as she lived in the early days of this poor old silly globe, no wonder they worshipped them as gods and goddesses!' he thought.

A sudden feverish longing arose to see her again soon, as soon as possible. Hal had certainly not been the master of his desires. He had been far nearer being their slave. Should he waive the interminable, stupid *table d'hôte*, and go off to the 'Weisse Rose' again? Pondering, he resolved that it was quite possible that he might be *de trop* there. No; he would not go.

'I will stay here and endure the bore,' he decided. 'If I am such a good boy to-night, I deserve reward to-morrow. Old Müller, the courier, doesn't mean us to start again till to-morrow evening. I may spend some hours with them before I go.'

Then he smoked away, dreaming of his next meeting with Griselda. He was de-

termined to reassert that right which had
become his by Mrs Black's dying request,
—the right to protect and care for sweet
Griselda. He blamed himself for having
drifted with the tide, for having allowed
himself to be almost estranged from his
little love all these years. But now was
the time. He would soon be of age
—his own master—and Griselda seemed
to be in a sore strait.

'If Black had private property, he
might write any number of Atheistical
books and come out all right,' he mused.
' But the poor beggar hasn't! So they are
all at his heels, like a pack of hounds.'

Hal was not good company for his
family that night. He sneered at everything. His father looked at him in mild
wonderment ; his mother held her head
high, and, attributing his ill humour to

'those Blacks,' comforted herself that they would be all far away up the Rhine in twenty-four hours out of 'those people's' path ; his sisters defended themselves by saying as many sharp things as they could in return for his teasing. Disagreeing constantly among themselves, they found that union was strength, and that it was necessary to make common cause against their spoiled elder brother, or, as Mabel expressed it, they would be 'nowhere.'

But next morning he was in a better temper. He seldom rose till noon, having accustomed himself to keep late hours. But to-day his breakfast was over, and he was out and traversing the bridge before twelve had struck from the church towers.

It was a pure, clear summer morning.

The great river rippled and danced in the sunshine. Boats went to and fro —the steam-ferry came throbbing across with its freight of a couple of gaily-dressed market-women and an old priest, who sat in the stern, his chin resting on his hands that were clasped upon his long staff. He had come from the requiem mass in the cathedral, and his dim eyes gazed vaguely out upon the stream, as he sat dreaming and wondering why a good, great man everyone had loved should have been suddenly snatched away, and he, poor, simple, old, useless body, left. Meanwhile, a big dog ran backward and forward on the quay, howling, barking, restlessly wagging his shaggy tail. The river lay between him and his master, who had gone across in the last ferry-boat. There seemed a curious mixture of joy and sor-

row in the scene about Hal—just as he felt
that there was in life. Perhaps, if he
had been ten years older, he would have
thought that trite thought—how ' all would
be the same a hundred years hence.'
But his young heart beat too passion-
ately, his young pulses were too active,
even vehement, for him to be passive.

As he went along, he swung his
cane, and his thoughts were busy about
'that poor old fellow,' as his youth
designated the Vicar's middle age. ' He
has had a hard fight, if all be
true,' he mused. Rumours anent John
Black's parentless state had reached
even to rural Crowsfoot. ' First, a
wretched boyhood, for fellows don't
mince matters in a public school, or
in a private one either; I expect he
must have had a bad time of it.

Then he was awfully fond of that
beautiful woman, his wife. I should
say all the love in his nature was
concentrated and given right over to
her. It must have been a frightful
blow when she died. Small wonder
it should shake his faith! It certainly
was a mistake to go and stick his
doubts into a book; for, as he de-
pends upon the Church for his income, it is quarrelling with his bread
and butter! But a man's making a
mistake is no reason for his friends
to turn their backs upon him — just
the contrary. At any rate, I sha'n't;
I can afford to stick by him, and
the governor can always be brought
to follow my lead — the mother too,
by a little management. Only those
women are not to be trusted. They'll

agree with you to your face, and,
the minute your back's turned, will
go plotting and planning against you.
There's no honour in them; they
don't know what it means. But
Griselda—well, she's not like a woman,
as I know women—that's all.'

The young fellow went on more
quickly. Then the 'Weisse Rose' came
into view. He slackened his steps,
and approached the quaint old hostelry,
—which occupied a corner where three
of the narrow, unsavoury streets met,—
more leisurely, as if he were saunter-
ing by. He did not wish to seem
hasty or undignified in Griselda's eyes.
And who could tell? She might be
looking out of a window. At that
very moment those great eloquent
eyes might be fixed upon him. It

was an uncomfortable sensation; and, as he walked towards the crooked building, with the overhanging second storey and the heavy wooden roof, he felt as if he had never before noticed what troublesome and un-graceful appendages arms and legs were, especially when you were trying to walk with unconscious airiness.

There was something wrong at the 'Weisse Rose.' As he neared the open door, he heard eager voices chattering away loudly in German. Then one of the fair-haired, blue-eyed wenches rushed out, cried, '*Ach—aber der liebe Herr!*' with a certain horror-stricken surprise, and rushed back again. Then, although Hal walked in and stamped about the little room where he had smoked and drunk with the Vicar of

Crowsfoot only yesterday, no one came
to him. He coughed, he knocked an
empty glass with his pocket-knife, he
whistled he even came out and cried,
' Hi—here—somebody!' He knew no
German. There was only a subdued
but eager muttering of that guttural language somewhere 'behind the scenes.'
No one answered his summons.

' This is a fine state of affairs!'
he said to himself, annoyed and
nettled at being, as he considered,
treated with disrespect. ' I do wonder at Black bringing his daughter
here.' Then he found a hand-bell,
and, walking out into the desolate bar,
rang till the red-faced landlord came out,
vociferating in German and gesticulating,
his bristly hair seeming to stand on end,
his eyes starting out of his head.

After a volley of what Hal considered 'gibberish,' the young man made the landlord of the 'Weise Rose' understand that he understood —nothing.

'Madame speek—leetle English,' he stammered. And, after a prolonged absence, during which Hal was disturbed by strange fears of he knew not what, the plump proprietress appeared, evidently greatly disturbed.

It was indeed a very little 'English' that she spoke. But, after great efforts on both sides, Hal learnt that something serious had come to pass since yesterday.

'De gentleman mad, mad!' said the woman. 'He try kill. We never 'ave so persons in die "Weisse Rose."' She almost thrust Hal out in her

excitement. He could find out nothing
further. He could not gather whether
Mr Black had gone suddenly crazy,
whether he and his daughter were
still there, or, indeed, what had taken
place. He tried to mount the crazy
little staircase, up which Griselda had
flitted after she bade him good-night the
previous evening. He was resolved to
know the worst at all costs ; but the
landlord came out, and he and his wife
jabbered in German, and opposed his
further entrance ; finally, by their united
efforts, pushing him towards and out
of the door, which, so soon as he was
fairly outside, they shut and barred against
him.

There he was, hustled, treated rudely,
if not roughly turned out into the street,
and in ignorance of what had happened

to Griselda and her father. It was more of an annoyance than a consolation to think that they had the companionship and assistance of Hugh Blunt.

'A fellow like that—who thinks of problems all day, and dreams of them all night—is simply useless in everyday life,' he thought. 'Oh, my poor Griselda, who said so sweetly that "girls had no troubles," what fresh burden has fallen upon you?'

He knocked at the bolted door of the inn; all remained quiet. He gazed up at the windows; they were blank. And, even as he looked, some one came and drew down the blinds.

'It strikes me that this is a case for the police,' Hal said to himself. 'Before half-an-hour is over, my good people, you shall be interrogated by someone against whom you dare not bar your doors.'

And he strode off, full of ardour, which was nevertheless tempered by a secret dread which he tried to hide from himself, but which grew stronger each moment.

CHAPTER VIII.

THE Rhine steamer *Der Edelmann* was steaming gaily up the river against wind and tide. A motley crowd of passengers was sitting on camp-stools or lounging on the benches under the awning. It was too hot to pace the deck. Only the little children ran about playing and chattering baby-talk, pretty little Parisians dressed in the height of fashion, attended by their neat white-capped *bonnes;* sturdy, stolid Germans; one or two English children, brought by venturesome parents. The ladies were knitting or reading newspapers and guide-books. The men stared about, yawned, smoked. Most of these tourists 'had seen it all before,' and were more interested in the vendors of the piles of purple plums or bunches of grapes, tastefully arranged with vine-leaves in flat, round baskets,—who came on board at one landing-place and left at the next,—than in the scenery.

Only one fair-haired girl stood leaning over the bulwarks, gazing steadfastly at the beautiful panorama. It was Griselda — a little plaid cloak half hiding her cotton dress. She was pale and sad. The great circles round her violet eyes showed fatigue. Yet, tired, miserable as she felt, the grand mountains rising solemnly before her, the forests of

vines that clung to the slopes at their
base, the rocky heights of the Drachen-
fels looming in the distance, appealed
to her love of the beautiful ; and as she
was borne slowly onwards against the
strong current of the rapid river, and
watched the ruined castles perched
among perilous crags up aloft, or the
red-roofed villages clustering down below among the green orchards, she felt
as if personal sorrow in such a scene
were scarcely sinless.

Yet she had good cause to be sorrow-
ful. Yesterday, after Hal Romayne left
them, her father opened letters from
England which had arrived while they
were out. The first was an imperative
demand from Mr Black's publisher for
the immediate settlement of all claims
for the unfortunate book, *Certain Pas-*

sages in Holy Writ Examined by a Clergyman of the Church of England, which, according to Messrs Cotton & Woolstone, of Paternoster Row, who had undertaken to publish the much-abused volume for its author, had proved as complete a financial as it had seemed to be a literary failure.

This Mr Black had read with a certain bitterness; but it would have disturbed him less had Messrs Cotton & Woolstone refrained from enclosing certain scurrilous reviews cut from papers ecclesiastical and secular, which had appeared since he left England. He had tossed these to Hugh Blunt, who laughed, and said,—

'You are just such a red flag to the Anglicans as Luther was to Rome.'

But the words were scarcely out of

the young man's mouth before John Black rose to his feet with the hoarse cry one hears sometimes from a wounded beast. Then he sank back in the chair from which he had risen — muttering and crying out — seized with sudden delirium.

His second letter was from his solicitors, Messrs Everest & Everest, curtly declining to make any further advances (he had drawn upon them according to their proposal ten years ago—this time for the education of his sons, Tom being at Cambridge and Harry in a surveyor's office), and giving as their reason his most peculiar position, openly attacking the religion whose emoluments provided his daily bread. Such a position, Messrs Everest considered, could scarcely be long maintained, and they regretted to state that, should the matter come into the Ecclesiastical Courts, they must decline acting for their whilom client in any way whatsoever.

The third letter was from his bishop,— a bitter, scornful epistle. He stated that, after consultation with supreme authority, he must call upon John to recant, to withdraw his work with public apology, and to disclaim his 'vain and profane disquisitions,' or take the consequences, which consequences, he assured him, meant as surely temporal ruin here as such profanity meant eternal ruin hereafter.

These sharp, unexpected blows upset the Vicar of Crowsfoot's weary brain. Fortunately for him, his daughter was as cool and collected as she was tender and loving, and Hugh Blunt, whose opinions were even more unorthodox than his tutor's, and who therefore heartily sympathised with him, proved a valuable nurse and help to Griselda. They at once summoned the first medical man in the German city, and in a few hours John Black was sufficiently recovered from his transient delirium to pursue his journey. The physician insisted upon change of scene. But even, had he not done so, out of the 'Weisse Rose' they must have gone; for the landlord, who had once before had some painful experiences with a lunatic, was frightened out of his wits, and was therefore to be to a certain extent excused for his churlish treatment of Hal Romayne that morning.

Hugh had been, as Griselda was grate-

fully thinking, while she gazed wonderingly at the great hills, at the soft
cloudlets poised in the rich deep blue
of a German sky—at the clear deeps of
the grand old river—well—he had been
everything to her these last twenty-four
hours. Remembering her brothers—selfish Tom and weak-willed Harry, the
only young men she had had any real
experience of — she wondered at the
self-control, thoughfulness, and delicate
sympathy of her father's pupil, who was
ordinarily 'short,' rough indeed, in his
manner.

He was now sitting by her father—
who had fallen into an uneasy doze,
stretched upon a cabin sofa. Hugh had
insisted upon Griselda's remaining on
deck. He had assumed a certain filial
and fraternal command, and, unaccus-

tomed as she was to resistance, she
meekly obeyed. Half-an-hour ago, she
had gone below to see how they were
getting on. Her father was asleep.
Hugh, sitting on a camp-stool, reading,
smiled and silently shook his head at
her. So she returned to her corner on
deck — where she was hidden by the
man at the wheel — and, turning her
back upon the little world on board,
faced the greater world of Nature.

Just as she was thinking of Hugh,
she heard his voice behind her.

' I have come to look after you.'

' How is he ? '

' Sleeping like an infant. I expect
it is the reaction. He is utterly ex-
hausted.'

' Was it not all—awful ? '

' Yes, it was,' said Hugh candidly,

leaning his elbows on the rail, and gazing
down into the cool green depth of the
rushing water. 'It was almost a fight.
I never expected he would rally so
soon. But what I feel about it is this,
Griselda : only one difficulty is over.
When his head is clear and steady again,
he must face the situation. How will
he do it? That shrewd old Doctor
Schwenk foresaw that. He said your
father had certainly weakened his brain,
either by overwork or loss of sleep. Of
course, I told him of impending trouble.
He said, in his old quaint way, "*Das
muss aber nicht sein*"; in which I
agreed, but asked, How could it be
averted? He gave me what schoolboys
call a "regular dressing." He asked me
what I thought I had been given youth
and strength for, and what you were for,

if not to act and make use of youth
and its powers when called upon. He
suggested I should assume the command.
I told him I was nobody—merely your
father's pupil. "Then you have helped
overtire this poor man's brain," he said,
"and you refuse to help it to rest?"
At this he looked at me through his
spectacles like some old owl, in a cynical
way I shall not easily forget; he evidently felt great contempt for me. I was
goaded into speaking out—' Hugh gave
a laboured sigh, and hesitated.

'What did you say?' Griselda spoke
gently. As Hugh spoke, her heart sank.
She had recognised Doctor Schwenk's
cleverness when he attended her father,
and she knew what his hints meant.

'I told him that I would lay down
my life for you and your father,' said

Hugh, his voice husky with suppressed emotion, 'but that interfere in such a matter I dared not. You, Griselda, you are the only one who can do anything. Your brothers — well, they mean well — but Tom is a fresh-man, and naturally rather raw, and — well, of course poor Harry, good-natured though he is, is of no earthly use in an affair of this kind.'

Griselda, her eyes fixed vaguely on the beautiful mountains, heard and understood that a great weight of responsibility was slowly settling down upon her young shoulders.

'What could I do?'

She clasped her hands, and looked earnestly up into Hugh's face. There was something so firm, so calm, in that hand-clasp, in that sweet but steadfast look, that, admiring her as Hugh had constantly admired her since he first saw Griselda in her simple home, he had never admired her as now.

'Your duty lies in a nutshell,' he said, trying to speak dryly. 'He is for the present, till his brain recovers power, incapable of acting for himself. You are his natural regent here ; now you must take the reins.'

They talked earnestly and long. Hugh simply stated what he thought must be done. They would continue travelling until the Vicar showed signs of recovery. He himself would furnish the ready money ; the Vicar could repay him any day. 'He is only too anxious to pay for and repay others,' he said. 'Money burns a hole in his pocket, as they say.' Hugh had no fear that his and Griselda's nursing among these exquisite scenes, where nature seemed constantly at work to excel herself, would bring health of mind and body to John Black.

Meanwhile, he suggested that Griselda should reply to those letters which had brought about the climax of her father's brain trouble.

He thought she should write to the publishers, the lawyers, and the bishop, stating that her father was seriously ill, but that, so soon as he would be sufficiently recovered, he would reply to their communications in person. Griselda was ready, but diffident.

'You must write simply, just as you feel,' said Hugh. 'I have no doubt but that it will be all right.'

Then he sent her down to sit by her father. He felt the want of being alone. Looking downwards into the clear, rushing water, where he could see the silvery fish and the green weeds carried along by the strong current, he drew in long breaths of the fresh, sweet air. It almost seemed to him as if he had not had time to breathe since Mr Black had been seized with that strange but happily short delirium — no, nor time to think — only time to feel.

Now, as he was gently carried along the great river, the mountains towering above — each minute bringing him face to face with one or another of Nature's works, all so beautiful that his progress was a series of surprises—he felt as one who is in an enchanting dream. Men and women may cheat themselves about themselves in every-day life ; but they are generally truthful in dreams. And even, as if in a dream, Hugh felt, now, that he loved this innocent young girl with the one love which moulds a man's life.

It was a revelation. For he had assured himself that he had a fraternal feeling, an honestly manly admiration for Griselda Black, but that this was all. He was merely beginning life, the eldest of a large family. And, although his father, the well-known Justice Blunt, was well off, he expected his sons to help themselves, and create their own careers, even as he had done. So Hugh Blunt would have no drag in the shape of a 'love-affair.' He had assured himself of this when he became Mr Black's pupil. As for a 'love-affair' with the grave young girl who presided with such old-fashioned simplicity over her father's household, he would as soon have thought of a 'love-affair' with the good-hearted but purblind and garrulous Jemima. He felt the chivalrous sensations when Griselda was in question that he felt when his own sisters were implicated. Yet to-day, here, after the night's violent excitement, seeing Rhineland for the first time, over-tired, unhinged, a moment when sober truth asserts herself, his heart said, ' I love her.'

The leap into life of a slumbering sen-sation, which he had not even suspected, was like any other shock. It stayed the ordinary, quiet course of his practical nature.

'Anyone would love her,' he said to himself almost angrily. He tried to per-suade himself that his feeling was great admiration, lively sympathy, deep, hon-est friendship. He partially succeeded. 'That stupid passion which rules boors, fools — the lowest of mankind — it is a desecration to connect it with her name and with mine,' he said to himself. 'As for me, I shall never marry ; and as for her—well, her life-work lies pretty plainly before her, and she is not one to shrink from it.'

Then he thought practically, tersely, of the situation. He was staunch, ready. He would not shirk one item of the immediate duty he considered specially his—that of nursing the Vicar of Crowsfoot until he regained his mental vigour.

He rejoined the father and daughter. Mr Black was awake, and calm. He arranged that they three should dine on deck while the *table-d'hôte* was proceeding below. He fee'd the waiter who was to attend upon them, in advance. He made his way to the kitchen, and had a brief but successful interview with the white-capped *chef*.

There had scarcely been a more deli-cately - arranged dinner on board *Der Edelmann* than this, which was served on the deserted deck that bright summer evening to the gaunt, pale clergyman, his anxious daughter, and the determined young man, Hugh Blunt.

As they ate and drank and talked, the Vicar occasionally relapsing into semi-vacuous thought, the giant shadows thrown across the river by the high hills deepened into darkness. Bright stars came out one by one on the dusky blue overhead. Then came the bustle of returning diners, the clatter of busy feet pacing the deck, sounds of music from the saloon below.

A deep stillness was settling down

upon the mountains, which were gradually growing black against a luminous sunset, when the steamer slackened speed, and stopped at the landing-place of Goarshausen, where Hugh thought it best they should stay a while.

It was a quiet little place. A few houses and two good-sized hotels glimmered white against the sombre background of wooded hills.

The Vicar walked from the pier to the hotel, leaning heavily on Hugh's arm. Griselda, following with the luggage-porter, noticed how her father stooped and tottered. She was deeply anxious. But, as she gazed up into the vast star-sprinkled heavens, the thought of the great universe with its multiplication of huge planets, brought that sense of her own insignificance, of the infinitesimal smallness of human beings, with their selfish hopes, fears, joys, and sorrows, which is a comfort to certain minds while suffering.

The 'Goldenes Kreuz' was a neat airy building, with a general aspect of polished floor, gleaming white china stoves, aloes and palms in huge red pots, shining white damask - covered tables, and flitting black forms, busy waiters deftly carrying high piles of covered plates, napkin on arm. The rooms allotted to the party were square, somewhat solemn apartments, overlooking the Rhine.

'I mean to get him to bed at once,' said Hugh to Griselda in an undertone, as the three mounted the slippery staircase (Hugh insisted upon, at least for to-night, sharing the Vicar's room), 'and, if you take my advice, you will go too. Remember, you have not been in bed since the day before yesterday.'

But Griselda had those fateful letters on her mind. Once shut into her quaint bedroom, with the massive, box-like bed looking uninviting to English eyes— almost as un-English as the species of milk-jug planted in a slop-basin on the mahogany table, which did duty as wash-stand—she felt disinclined for bed, and as far from sleep as if she had but just risen from a long night's rest.

She unpacked her writing - desk and re-read the three letters which had had such a terrible effect upon her father.

There — in the calm silence, the Rhine splashing against the pebbly river - bank below, the murmuring of voices, the rustle of a dress, the crackling of a footstep audible in the wide stillness—Griselda, her elbows poised on the polished surface of the round table in the centre of the room, pored over those letters once more, and seemed to receive and assimilate their bitterness.

No, she could not sleep till they were replied to. The question was, How to do it?

Griselda had not practised the art of correspondence. The few letters she had written had not taxed her faculty for composition. She had occasionally written to her brothers. She had written letters at her father's dictation, and even from notes jotted down by him.

All these years John Black had done his utmost to educate his daughter. Of course he refused that obnoxiously-worded offer of Lady Romayne's, that

arrived so inopportunely at the time of
his wife's death—the offer to lend him
the children's governess, without payment,
two or three days weekly. The Vicar
was weak in modern languages, ' but
she will do with what I can teach her,'
he resolved. Griselda had learnt Latin,
Greek, Algebra, Euclid, as her brothers
had. Perhaps this mental training had
helped to preserve that quaint simplicity
which made some persons call her 'odd,'
and others 'stupid.' The Vicar had
allowed her to read much bygone litera-
ture, that he particularly liked. But now,
at this juncture, little of her training
seemed of use. In a puzzled, anxious
way, she went to the windows and
leaned out, gazing at the rippling river
studded with star-reflections. Two men
— Englishmen — were walking up and

down below, in the hotel garden. Their cigar-ends were spots of red light in the darkness. As Englishmen will, with some notion that their language cannot leap the Channel, they spoke loudly and without reserve. They were talking of some acquaintance. One said to the other impatiently,—

'What could you expect? Anyone who cannot face a situation must look for ruin. Such creatures ought to be strangled, or put out of the way somehow by Act of Parliament. They are more useless and more of a nuisance than these abominable gnats.'

It was a chance—a coincidence, perhaps—that brought those men within earshot of Griselda just when she had 'to face a situation'—an important one for her father.

'Such creatures as I am, while I am a coward about writing, ought' — she paused to recall the exact words — 'ought to be strangled—put out of the way. They are more useless and more of a nuisance than those gnats. Oh dear! What a very peremptory man that must be! I am glad I don't know him. What would he think of me?'

Poor Griselda bit her lip as she remembered Tom's threat when she was but a baby-girl—that, if she would not obey him in this or that, he would wring her neck. 'I wonder why our poor necks are so badly treated?' she thought, instinctively protecting her soft fair throat with her hands. 'They used to be hacked at with an axe; now they dislocate them with a rope.'

Then she turned bravely back to her

desk, and began the worst first, the letter to the bishop.

Hugh had said, 'Write simply—just as you feel.'

'Well, I couldn't do anything else ; I am not clever enough,' she told herself, as she resolutely mended a pen and began,—

'GOARSHAUSEN, *August* —, 18—.

'MY LORD,—Your letter to my father has made him very ill. It is true that it arrived by the same post as one from his publisher, asking payment for printing his book, and one from his lawyers, saying that they could not advance him any more money. But those letters would not have brought on this brain-attack, for he is accustomed to disagreeable letters about money-matters. It was

your lordship's letter that he talked of
in his delirium. I cannot think what he
will do about this when he gets well ;
but one thing I do know, that, whatever
he wrote in that book, he will never
withdraw, for each word and sentence,
each thought, came from his heart,—and
if, when convinced, he were to deny his
convictions, he would be false to God
and to himself, which my father will
never be.

'We are doing our best to make him
well, when we shall immediately return
to England. As soon after as possible,
my father will call upon your lordship at
the palace, and I am,—Obediently yours,

'GRISELDA BLACK.'

Without daring to read over what she
had written, she took another sheet, and

in a few dignified words informed the publishers, Messrs Cotton & Woolstone, that the Vicar was indisposed, but would reply to their communication as soon as it was prudent for him to write. Then she laid this aside, and prepared to address Messrs Everest & Everest.

This was a more difficult matter. She sat biting the feather of her pen and reading that letter of theirs over and over again.

'If I told them the truth,' she thought, 'it would be that they are cold-blooded, and that I think them cowards for thrusting their help upon him when he did not want it, and suddenly withdrawing it just when he wants help more, I expect, than he ever wanted it in his life. No; I must write the merest commonplaces to those lawyers.'

She dashed off a note in her boldest handwriting—

'To Messrs Everest & Everest.

'SIRS,—Your communication addressed to my father, the Rev. John Black, reached him in Germany; I, his daughter, reply for him, as he is at present too ill to write, or indeed to be consulted about business at all. As soon as he may with prudence undertake the management of his affairs again, he will consider the contents of your letter, and will most likely forward you his reply ; and I am, sirs,—Yours, etc.,   GRISELDA BLACK.'

She felt satisfied with ' yours, etc.'—it might mean anything. Griselda had an antipathy for—something akin to a fear of—these lawyers, the Everests. Young

child that she was when she first heard
their names, she was observant ; and she
soon found out that her father depended
upon them in some way. He either returned from a visit to their offices in
high spirits, or moody and distrustful.

If, as she undressed and crept wearily
to bed, worn out with fatigue, anxiety,
and the natural excitement of a first visit
abroad among all the beautiful strange
sights and sounds, she could have guessed,
even in some degree, what her father's
actual connection with the Lincoln's Inn
solicitors really was!

But, as the moonlight crept in and lay
in blue-white patches on the polished
floor—as strange shadows, cast by passing clouds flitting across the night sky
or by the tree-branches waving in the
warm wind—flickered mysteriously upon

the walls, she fell into a sleep untroubled by dream or vision.

She did not even think once of 'to-morrow'—to-morrow, which was to kindle a fire in her gentle soul which could only die when that soul fled from her body—perhaps not even then!

END OF VOL. I.

COLSTON AND COMPANY, PRINTERS, EDINBURGH.